TALL JERRY

Ireland

# TALL JERRY

AND THE

# DELPHI FALLS TRILOGY

ECHOED LEGENDS

## Legend Three

## TALL JERRY

*in*

## *Heaven Sends for Hemingway*

First Edition

# JEROME MARK ANTIL

ISBN-13: 978-1-7326321-9-6 (Paperback)
ISBN-13: 978-1-7326321-6-5 (Trilogy Set)

Library of Congress Control Number: 2019904865

SCENE: RURAL AMERICA
TIME: POST WAR 1953
(Thanksgiving week.)

Historical references offered by
Judy Clancy Conway; Marty Bays; Dale Barber;
New Woodstock Historical Society; Cincinnatus NY Historical Society;
Pompey NY Historical Society; Cortland NY Historical
Society; Cazenovia Public Library; Carthage NY Historical
Society; Binghamton NY Historical Society

Some characters are made from combinations of Jerry's siblings
(James, Paul, Richard, Frederick, Michael, Dorothy, and Mary)

PRINTED IN AMERICA

# TABLE OF CONTENTS

*12-year-old Tall Jerry, his mom and dad. 1953*

Legends of Tall Jerry in the Delphi Falls Trilogy are of a time filled with characters that show true heroism. Of legends that happened after the war and before there were cell phones and an internet, and not every house had a telephone or television. Of a time when a full, hot meal at school cost a quarter. The people are real, and the fictionalized legends are based in truth, give or take a stretch or two. The Delphi Falls with its shale-crusted cliffs, big white rock, my boyhood home, campsite and barn garage are there to see today if you have a mind to head on up to the town of Cazenovia, New York—near the hamlet of Delphi. Both waterfalls are magical to this day, I promise. Oh, they may not grant a wish or turn tin into gold, but they will make you feel good about yourself and give you confidence.

JMA

*The Jim Crow south.*

*(Library of Congress archives)*

# CHAPTER 1

# A LETTER TO DELPHI FALLS FROM
# LITTLE ROCK, ARKANSAS

## NOVEMBER 22, 1953

*Dear Dad,*

*Can you please telephone Mom here and tell her I'm 12 and I'm old enough to ride on a Greyhound bus alone? Please Dad? I want to come home. I hate Arkansas. It is scary. Get me out of here. Please, please, please.*
*Call Mom and tell her.*

*Love,*
*Jerry*

# CHAPTER 2

## IT WAS A SIGN

Something mean in howls of the wind this night. Threatening it was, with ole Charlie setting on a limb hanging over the creek up between the two Delphi Falls. I was meditating an early evening prayer when the upper falls got my full attention with a bolder from its top breaking loose and crashing down at the foot of the falls trying to tell me something. A bolt of white lightning struck the stone midair and rode it down to its perdition. The rock flashed brightly at the bottom, and I could see the two waterfalls looking at me, as if they both had eyes and were trying to say something to me. With another crack, lightning struck the rock a second time, sending it flying, while another electric bolt lit up, ricocheting off it and veering into the shale side of the cliff.

Legend three was stirring, and ain't no better place than Delphi Falls for legends to brew.

Ole Charlie here enjoys the solitude setting on a branch above and behind the first falls in the rain with a view down to Tall Jerry's house and the barn garage, water pounding and lightning crashing all sides of me.

November had so far been a month of golden sunsets, full-wafer moons, a brisk scarf and sweater cold. The brilliant reds, yellows, burnt oranges, and the smell of chimney smoke reminded folks of minced meat pie, turkey stuffing and cranberry jams.

Flying Eddie made it home and was working at a bakery in Binghamton. He'd carve a turkey this Thanksgiving. Missus drove

Dick and Tall Jerry to Little Rock to help out while their aunt Mary has a new baby.

Lightning cracked again, this time splitting the tree I was sitting on like a pickaxe clear through the middle. Half the tree trunk and my branch were left standing, the other half splashing down into the creek. The ground was shaking while the trunk floated over the falls and into Tall Jerry's backyard.

Until this storm, all had been quiet in the Crown. This was a sign.

*Big Mike at Delphi Falls walks to the docs.*

# CHAPTER 3

## IT HAD TO START SOMEWHERE

Big Mike wasn't "in his cups" the Saturday he walked from the Delphi Falls over to the doc's, but by the look in his eyes and the bottle of bourbon in his hand, he had something weighty on his mind. As the doc's barn door opened, he waited as the Jeep backed out. He flagged him to stop and talk a spell. The doc obliged. Big Mike leaned on the Jeep, stretched his long right arm and set the bourbon bottle on the hood while his left hand pulled on his silky dark blue tie to loosen it from its knot. He unbuttoned his shirt collar. As a courtesy to his friend, the doc turned the engine off, figuring his run to Hasting's for cabbages and pipe tobacco could wait.

"Did Missus, Dick, and Tall Jerry make it to Little Rock?" the doc asked.

"They've been there several days, Doc," Big Mike said.

"Long drive, Arkansas," the doc said.

"Missus took the boys to help Aunt Mary Thanksgiving week, as she's about to have a baby."

"This her first?" the doc asked.

"Her fourth. The boys will help with the little ones. Missus will help when the baby comes home."

The doc understood that it was pretty much common country knowledge that a family man like Big Mike left setting at the supper table all alone too many nights in the empty church quiet of dairy-farm country was prey to certain apparitions and depressions in the head. Big Mike for one didn't favor being alone all that much ever since his one-year or so stretch in the tuberculosis sanatorium, but

5

it seemed this day, with carrying a bottle of bourbon to the doc's, he had something other than country loneliness gnawing on his mind. Just then the general-store owner, Mike Shea, was driving by. He saw them both, his friends Big Mike and Doc, and pulled his car over and rolled his window down.

"Hey Mike," Big Mike said.

"Howdy," Mike Shea said.

"You lost, Mike?" the doc quipped.

"Just out for a drive, looking for a friendly game of pitch."

He turned the engine off and poked an ear out his car window to listen.

Big Mike started a story of being asked to join the country club in Cortland and how he mentioned the fancy invite to friends at the bakery and learned the country club didn't take Italians, Jews, or Africans as members.

"None of the above?" Mike Shea asked.

"Imagine my hearing it from friends at the bakery—a Jew, an Italian, and an African?" Big Mike asked.

"I wonder what they would have said had you asked them first?" Mike Shea asked.

"Why would I ask them? They're friends. They aren't colors, races, or religions to me. They're friends."

"I could see how it could get your goat, I sure enough could," Mike Shea said.

"Made me cringe—or *bristle* might be a better word."

"What'd you do?" the doc asked.

"I left the bakery in a stomp, told myself that buying a fifth of Kentucky bourbon might ease my burn."

"It wouldn't hurt," Mike Shea grinned.

"I drove home, parked, and walked over here to Doc's place to blow off some steam."

"Big Mike," the doc said. "The sneaky, persnickety ways at a club like that proves it's filled with pantywaists. It's been pretty much an embarrassment for some time."

"It shouldn't come as any surprise," Mike Shea said.

"I guess I knew it, deep down. I just didn't want to believe it."

"They're not secret about it," Mike Shea said.

Mike Shea stepped out of his car, stood and rested his elbow on top of the opened driver door.

"Big Mike, I've known you for—what's it been now, since the thirties?"

"1931. I called on your store to sell you bread," Big Mike said.

"You two have known each other that long?" the doc asked.

"It was Mike who told me about the Delphi Falls in 1938. That's when I bought it," Big Mike said.

"I first met Big Mike when he and his partner started the bakery in '31," Mike Shea said.

"You two go back," the doc said.

"That's why I have a feeling there's something in his craw," Mike Shea said. "I know you and something tells me it's not a country club that isn't worth spit in the bigger scheme of things."

"Ya think?" Big Mike asked, lifting the bottle from the hood.

"They've been hiding behind a dress code for years."

"Looks that way," Big Mike said.

"What's on your mind? You're among friends," the doc said.

"You can tell the doc here and me," Mike Shea said.

Big Mike took a swig of bourbon and swallowed with a squeeze of his eyelids.

"I got a letter and a postcard from my boy today. It's just that I was thinking about it, is all. His letter and postcard."

"A letter and postcard on the same day," Mike Shea said.

"Which boy?" the doc asked.

"Jerry."

"Tall Jerry," Mike Shea said. "Sounds serious."

Big Mike pulled the postcard from his back pocket. He held it up. "Look how he addressed it. To Big Mike, New Woodstock, NY.

*Dad, when my letter I sent gets there, can you give it to Mary Crane? I marked it PHBC—secret! Did you get my other letter? PS, I don't like Arkansas. Jerry."*

"It's the 'I don't like Arkansas that's bothering you," Mike Shea said.

"What do you mean?" the doc asked.

"Big Mike saw it, Doc—the prejudice—firsthand in Cortland today, and now he's waking up to the way things have been for years."

Big Mike took another swig.

"I got a letter from him begging to come home and now this."

"Your boy is seeing Jim Crow down south," the doc said.

"I know he is," Big Mike said.

"You know what it's like there, and it bothers you Tall Jerry might be in the thick of it all," the doc said.

"Are we close to the button?" Mike Shea asked.

Big Mike nodded, remembering his young adventures.

"I traveled through the south on my way to Louisiana and Texas back in the 1920s. I wanted to see my Acadian roots."

"You a Frenchy, Big Mike?" the doc asked.

"Normandy through Canada."

"I knew Missus is full Irish," the doc said.

"I'll never forget it," Big Mike said. "It seemed some people in the south would look right through other people almost like they didn't exist."

"And you're wondering what Tall Jerry's seeing for the first time," Mike Shea said.

"The boy's resilient," the doc said. "Have a sit-down with him when he gets home. Tall Jerry's a smart kid. Just let him know it's not the way things are most places."

Big Mike leaned in.

"In 1922, I was at a Greyhound station stop for sandwiches in Arkansas. I saw a drugstore about thirty miles from the Mississippi," Big Mike said.

"What's your point?" Mike Shea asked.

"The drugstore had a six-inch square flap door in its brick alley wall. If an African needed a prescription, they weren't allowed in the drugstore. They had to poke their arm through the hole, money in hand and wait for someone to put the medicine in their hand."

"Tall Jerry's a strong lad," Mike Shea said. "He'll see the wrong."

"Just have a talk with him," the doc said.

Big Mike slid the postcard back into his pocket and reached for the bottle, pulled its cork and lifted it.

"Tell me this," he asked. "Why didn't I drive back to the club and give them a piece of my mind, like a man? I just bought a bottle of bourbon and drove home in a sulk."

He took another swig of bourbon.

"It's 'cuz all those country-club members and their businesses buy a lot of bread, pies, and cakes, maybe?" Mike Shea asked.

Big Mike pursed his lips and nodded, knowing Mike Shea had a point—that men protect their own interests. He set the bottle down. Nobody spoke for a spell. Big Mike stared off at a hill behind the doc's barn before he spoke again.

"Hundreds of years of slavery have shredded America's moral fiber. Our conscience has been torn like an Achilles tendon," Big Mike said.

Mike Shea closed his car door behind him and motioned Big Mike to hand him the bottle. After tipping it back, he lowered the bottle while gritting a whiskey-wrenched swallow.

9

"You may have to drive me back to my store, Doc. You'd better not drink so you're able. Just smoke your pipe."

He took another snort, shivered his head and handed the bottle to Big Mike.

"Abolition came, gentlemen. It took a while, but it came," the doc said. "Bully for Lincoln, and bully for abolition! We finally got it right!"

"I don't think you're getting what the man's trying to say, Doc," Mike Shea said.

"What am I missing?" the doc asked.

"Abolition came all right, but it came without absolution."

"Now what in the hell does that mean?" the doc growled.

"Abolition without any absolution was like putting a bandage on over four hundred years of slave ownership—people owning people. Ain't that right, Big Mike?" Mike Shea asked.

Big Mike nodded his head.

Doc pushed his hat brim up with his thumb and scratched his hairline.

"I'm just a dentist. Either of you care to explain that to me?"

"Doc, the abolition vote was good—I'm not doubting that for a second," Mike Shea said.

"Well, there you go," the doc said.

"But signing it with no follow-up is like hanging mistletoe over an open doorway to freedom," Mike Shea said.

"As if freedom and acceptance were light switches you could flip on and off," Big Mike said.

Big Mike took a snort, sucked air through his teeth and handed the bottle to Mike Shea. He stared at the ground for balance, thinking back on his Greyhound bus travels around America as a young man.

"The America with a conscience embraced abolition; the America without one considered it mistletoe."

"I don't get it," the doc said.

"Poison," Big Mike said.

10

"Is mistletoe poisonous?" Mike Shea asked.

"The berries could kill you."

"I still don't get it," the doc said. "Wasn't abolition—freeing people—what we wanted?"

Mike Shea raised his fist gently to his chest, lowered his chin, puffed his cheeks, and muffled a belch.

"We never said we were sorry, Doc."

"What!?"

"I like that," Big Mike said.

"We passed abolition, freedom for all, without any education, Doc. The folks we freed couldn't read and write because they weren't allowed to when they were slaves. We opened the gates and let them loose to feed and fend for themselves, like free-range chickens."

"We didn't educate freed slaves. Is that what you're going on about?" the doc asked.

"It's worse, Doc," Mike Shea said.

"What could be worse than owning a person?" the doc asked.

"We didn't educate America," Big Mike said.

"We didn't educate anybody," Mike Shea said.

Big Mike set the bottle on the hood.

"Fifty-six thousand people were murdered at the Buchenwald death camp during the war in Germany," Big Mike said.

"I don't get the connection," the doc said.

"General George Patton ordered the German civilians in towns near that camp to march five miles up a hill, escorted by armed American soldiers, to see the stacks of bodies. It took two days for the Weimar residents to file through the camp."

"General Patton wanted townspeople to see what they had turned their backs on throughout the war," Mike Shea said.

"So, what you're saying is we turned our backs on slavery as a country."

"And now we're turning our backs on Jim Crow," Mike Shea said.

The doc took a puff on his pipe and stared off at a tree.

"How do we apologize for something like that?"

"We spent hundreds of years setting bad examples, teaching grade school children wrong by those examples," Big Mike said.

"Had we spent the years since the Civil War teaching grade school children and different cultures and what's right would have been our saying we're sorry," Mike Shea said.

"How would that do it?" the doc asked.

"The kids in the 1860s would have integrated on their own steam." Big Mike said.

"This sort of thing can only be taught," Mike Shea said.

Big Mike's loneliness melted, sobered him enough to cork the bottle and walk back on home and lie down.

Doc and Mike Shea walked across to the doc's house to play a few hands of pitch.

Ole Charlie here watched over Big Mike. He was a remarkable man. He was a lad of thirteen and nearly fully grown when his father fell from the barn roof. He quit school and walked from Minnesota to North Dakota to work wheat fields, hands calloused from leather reins as he drove teams of four pulling wheat thrashers. All the while, he sent money home to help his mother.

*Big Mike at thirteen in 1915 in North Dakota*

Big Mike would climb and sit on top of a Black Hills mountain and sing,

"*Oh, give me a home where the buffalo roam, and the deer and the antelope play,*" just as loud as he could to hear his echoes sing back as he watched the stars.

Now in the kitchen waiting on the coffee percolator, Big Mike tapped the postcard on his palm like he was playing the snare drum in a dirge at a Frenchman's wake. Tall Jerry was away from the state for the first time at twelve and wanted to come home. Big Mike was thirteen when he first traveled out of state. Maybe the postcard from Jerry warranted a telephone call, so he could talk about prejudices the lad is seeing in Little Rock. He looked out the back window at the lower waterfall and remembered there were no telephones when he traveled the states at thirteen. Maybe it'd be best Tall Jerry face it and not run away.

He poured the bourbon into the sink and dropped the empty in the trash. He stepped into the bedroom, pausing at the doorway, gathering his thoughts. He sat on the edge of the bed in the dark and picked up the receiver.

"Operator."

"Myrtie, I need the Cranes' on the wire, please."

"Are they young Mary's folks, Crane?"

"Yes, ma'am. Up near Watervale."

"Did Missus get to Arkansas?"

"It was a long drive, but they made it in time."

"Has the baby come?"

"Not yet—maybe tomorrow."

"Here you go."

"Thanks, Myrtie."

"Hello?"

"Betty, this is Mike."

"Did Missus make it to Little Rock?"

"They did. A postcard came with a message Jerry wants me to get to Mary."

"Mary's up the road with Aunt Lucy. She's helping get her house ready for a social. She's having friends in on Sunday."

"Aunt Lucy? Is she your sister?"

Mrs. Crane chuckled.

"No relation, she goes by Aunt Lucy. She bought the Ryan place a few houses up and lives in it on weekends and her days off. She's a live-in housekeeper for a doctor's family up in Syracuse and asks Mary and a friend for help with dishes, setting the table, serving at her party—that sort of thing. It's extra money for them, but I don't think they take it."

"There's a letter coming from Jerry. It's secret, his postcard says."

"A secret message, eh?" Mrs. Crane mused. "Sounds like here they go again."

"Knowing the boy, if he took time to hand-write a letter, it's important to him."

"Well, of course it is."

"Tell Mary I'll make spaghetti whatever night his letter gets here. The club might as well meet here at the falls where there's light to read by instead of the cemetery with kerosene lanterns. Besides, it's getting cold."

"I'll tell her."

"I could use the company."

"You're not with family for Thanksgiving, Big Mike?"

"They'll be in Little Rock. Thanksgiving is the busiest time of the year for the bakery, with bread stuffing, holiday pies, and all."

"You're welcome to come here."

"Thank you, Betty, but young Mike and his girlfriend will be home from Le Moyne. He's cooking our bird."

"Is that the brother Tall Jerry calls 'Gourmet Mike?'"

"One and the same. I'm sure he'll come up with some twist on a traditional Thanksgiving meal."

"Did Missus have business down there?"

"The boys' aunt lives there. They have a baby due any day now. They needed a hand with their little ones still in diapers, so Missus took Jerry and Dick to help out."

"They'll have their hands full."

"She's already gone full term. She'll be in the hospital four or five days when the baby comes and Don has to work."

"I'll let Mary know. I know they love your spaghetti."

The call ended, edging Delphi Falls closer to the holiday.

*Big Mike - age 13, singing to the echoes. (1915)*

## CHAPTER 4

## CAN'T HAVE BEEN NEAR DELPHI FALLS AND NOT KNOW THE STORY

On Saturday morning the telephone rang at Mary's house.

"Hello?"

"Is Mary there?"

"Hold on, honey, I'll get her."

Through the earpiece Barber could hear the clap of a screen door closing, followed by loud foot stomping, a ritual when wet grass or autumn leaves stuck to shoes.

"Hello," Mary said.

"D'ja go to the dance?"

"No, un-uh. Why?"

"No reason."

"Who is this?"

"Barber."

"You called to ask me that?"

"No."

"Why'd you ask it?"

"Never mind."

"Must be a reason you asked it."

"I didn't…"

"Boys don't bring up a dance after the dance for no reason."

"My mom—" Barber started.

"It's a girl, isn't it?"

"What?!"

Mary sang.

"Barber likes a girl…Barber likes a girl…"

"Shut up."

"And you want to know who she danced with and if she smooched, right?"

Silence reigned.

"Who is she?"

No answer.

"Tell me."

No answer.

"I promise I won't tell."

Mary was getting nowhere. Barber had hoped for more decorum from the club's president.

"Mom told me you called," Barber said. "You want me to set up a meeting?"

"Sort of, but not yet," Mary said.

"Huh?"

"Oh, all right, go ahead."

"Set it up or not?"

"Call everybody and tell them to be ready for a meeting."

"For when?"

"I don't know yet."

"Mary, you're making no sense."

"We're doing spaghetti at Big Mike's, either tonight or tomorrow night. It depends on when a letter gets here."

"When's it coming?"

"I'm waiting for Big Mike to call and tell me."

"A letter?"

"A letter."

"Tall Jerry sent a letter?"

"Yes, will you call?"

"Roger Wilko," Barber said.

"Good."

"What's the letter about—did anybody say?"

"We're getting a letter is all I know."

The two hung up and it wasn't ten minutes before Mary telephoned Barber.

"Set it up for tonight. Let's meet at Farmer Parker's at five."

"We're going to eat at Farmer Parker's?"

"No, we'll go see him first, make sure he's doing okay, then we'll walk over to Big Mike's for supper and read the letter."

They were in their teens, except for twelve-year-old Tall Jerry, but club procedures they'd set and spat on when they were eight, nine, and ten still stood. It was because of this unconditional respect for one another that the club worked. Even running Farmer Parker's farm when he wrenched his back and was laid up. They buried his dog.

Holbrook was so early he climbed to his and Tall Jerry's camp over the falls for a short nap before the meeting.

Mr. Vaas braked slowly at first and then ground a gear as he turned the '42 Dodge milk-can hauler into the driveway. The truck sounded like a lion's purr, rocking in idle, its diesel engine roaring, rattling Farmer Parker's toolshed and the tools inside clanking on the wall hooks. Randy, Mayor, and Mary piled out before he backed out and left.

Mr. Barber's gray Packard was the last to pull in. Its whitewall tires rolled majestically onto the drive, and Bases and Barber climbed out. Barber took his dad's keys, stepped around back, opened the trunk, and lifted out packages wrapped in butcher paper and tied with string. After shutting the trunk lid, he handed the keys back to Mr. Barber.

"If it's not late, bub, I'll pick you up," Mr. Barber said. "If you're late, hitch a ride or walk."

Farmers were at their best after a night's sleep. Their days started as early as four in the morning.

They gathered in the barn and said politeness's to Farmer Parker while he stripped a cow. Satisfied that things were fine with the old

19

man, they walked to the house. Mrs. Parker was rolling dough for holiday pies and had a bowl filled with the mix for a Christmas fruit-cake. Mary mentioned how lovely her roses were this late season, and she gave Mary a taste of jam.

"The secret is cutting them back before snowfall," she said. "After Thanksgiving I'll be trimming them…just a tad. It'll give the branches a chance come spring rain and sun."

After paying their respects, they moved in a single file down the worn walking path on the north side of the house and left of the wood plank bordering the strawberry patch. They stepped off the lawn one at a time, crossed the road and headed up the long dirt drive to Tall Jerry's house at the Delphi Falls.

"Farmer Parker must be lonely milking without Buddy," Mary said.

"I don't see why," Holbrook said. "Buddy was too old to go to the barn for more than a year. Why would he be lonely?"

"I don't know. Buddy was on the porch to say hello to him when he went down to the barn and hello again when he came back up," Mary said.

"Now he's dead and buried and Farmer Parker with no dog to greet him," Randy said.

"He told us he couldn't replace Buddy," Holbrook said.

"You want to get him another dog, don't you, Mary?" Barber asked. "I can smell it."

"Let's find him one before Christmas," Mary said. "We'll give it to him early."

*Looking down from the white rock at Delphi Falls.*

## CHAPTER 5

## MARY READS THE SECRETS

Big Mike held the screen door open, pulled an apron off and handed it to Mary.

"Make yourselves at home. Start your meeting—meet as late as you'd like. I forgot sausage. I'm going to pop over to Hasting's. We'll eat in about an hour or so."

Big Mike handed Mary the letter from Jerry, walked to his car, and drove off.

Stepping into the house, Holbrook beamed smelling the aromas of oregano, green peppers in a garlic-tomato sauce wafting about, and hints of the Italian sausage on its way. Big Mike's Italian sausage was Holbrook's favorite food.

Gathering at the table they selected chairs, leaving the head for Big Mike out of respect.

"Anybody have anything to say before I read the letter?" Mary asked.

"Mom sent packages for Aunt Lucy," Barber said. "For her Christmas charity."

"I didn't know you had an Aunt Lucy," Randy said.

"She lives up the road from Mary," Barber said. "Mary, tell her the packages are from Gertrude. She'll know."

Mary set the packages on the floor.

"If you're walking to her place, I think she's only home on Saturday and Sunday," Barber said.

"I know," Mary said. "I work for her sometime."

"Is she the lady Tall Jerry and I put up a clothesline for?" Holbrook asked.

"That's her," Mary said.

"My mom knows her."

"Who is she?" Mayor asked.

"Just a friend," Mary said. "She works in Syracuse. She collects clothes and cookware to give to charity."

"Whatever people donate, she wraps like Christmas presents and sends them to the needy," Barber said.

"She's not my aunt," Mary said. "She's a friend."

Mary looked around the table.

"Anybody got anything else?"

"Go ahead and read Tall Jerry's letter," Mayor said.

"Read it," Holbrook said.

"Read the letter," Randy said.

Mary started a rip in the envelope flap with a fingernail and lifted out pages folded in half and in half again. She unfolded them and pressed them to the tabletop with her palms. She puffed a curl from her eye.

"Here goes."

She thumbed through the pages without speaking.

"What are you waiting for?" Holbrook asked.

"I don't see a 'dear,'" Mary said.

"What?" Mayor asked.

"I'm looking for the beginning. I can't find 'dear' anywhere."

"Just start on the page on top. We'll figure it out," Barber said.

Mary shrugged and began reading.

*It's hot here but probably snowing up where you guys are in Delphi Falls, I bet. People talk with an accent. My mom calls it a drawl. Mom says everything's so hot people talk slower. It's like how they talk faster in Boston because it's so cold there, she said. Something like that. My aunt don't have enough beds with all their kids, so I have to sleep on a cot in the empty apartment on the second floor. The apartment owner said it was okay for me to sleep up there on an army cot. It's scary all alone in the dark. It's not like I can build a campfire up here. I know how to change a diaper now and I've been trying to get Don to tell me stories about when he flew his B-17 from England over Germany and dropped bombs in the war, but he works a lot. His guys bombed Hitler, Aunt Mary told me. She showed me the picture album of him in uniform and a picture he took out his window on a bombing mission. She told me his plane was Lady Helene and showed me pictures.*

Big Mike came in and made his way around the table.

"Don't stop, young lady. I'll be in the kitchen."

"Where was I?"

"His plane was *Lady Helene*," Randy said.

Mary continued.

*But that's not what I want to tell you guys. Dick and I took a bus to downtown Little Rock. We got off at the zoo, and that was fun, but then he showed me how some people in Arkansas aren't allowed to do everything other people can do. They call some people a name here, but it isn't polite, my mom says.*

"They do in Syracuse, too," Bases mumbled.

"Shut up!" Holbrook said. "Read, Mary!"

"My dad told me," Bases added.

Mary continued.

*Down here they have drinking fountains like we have at school, but they're outdoors here because it's so hot, but they*

24

*always have two. Know why? One has a sign on it that says who can drink at it and who can't. We even wanted to go to a movie and sit in the balcony, but they wouldn't let us. Know why? The ticket lady told us the balcony was for certain people only. She said that out loud where everybody around could hear her.*

"He'd better be careful," Mayor said. "I think they have laws down there that are different than the laws up here—they've still got laws from Civil War days."

"Maybe they put the drinking-fountain signs up for slaves and someone forgot to take them down after the Civil War," Bases said.

"Give me a break!" Mary said.

"I know they have the KKK all over the place—at least that's what I heard," Barber said. "They're nothing to mess with."

"Tall Jerry better tell Dick not to be mouthing off at anybody down there," Holbrook said.

Mary found her spot on the page and read on.

*Will somebody send me the master code sheet we made up for David Eisenhower, just in case I write a secret message? Ask my dad where to mail it or look on this envelope. Make sure my name is on the envelope when you mail it. That's all for now, but it is scary here. Tall Jerry*

*PS: Tell Holbrook I took my knapsack in case he's looking for it to go camping, but tell him to ask my dad for some food to take up. He can use my pillowcase to carry it. Tell him the Spam is in the cabinet over the icebox.*

Mary looked up. "He wants the master code," she said.

"Where is it?" Mayor asked.

"Does Duba still have it?" she asked.

"I think he had it last," Bases said.

"I wonder why he wants it," Mayor said.

"I'll ask Duba for it," Randy said.

"I think there's something he's afraid to tell us without a code," Barber said.

"Didn't Duba give the code master to Marty in case he needed it when we caught the pickpocket?" Mayor asked. "I'll ask Marty."

Big Mike came in, wiping his hands with a kitchen towel.

"I put the spaghetti in to boil," he said. "I have a few minutes before serving and couldn't help overhearing. Mind if I sit in?"

Big Mike was welcome but asked as a courtesy.

"Is it like that down there?" Holbrook asked.

"You mean in Arkansas?" Big Mike asked.

"Yes," Holbrook said.

"It's like that, in different sorts of ways, in many places," Big Mike said.

"Not in Syracuse," Bases said.

Big Mike sat and looked Bases in the eye.

"Son, there's a football player who Syracuse University won't give a football scholarship to this year because of his skin color. Among the best young high school athletes in America. His name is Jim Brown. You'll be reading about him, I'm sure. They didn't want him because of his race."

"For real?" Holbrook asked.

"For real. He's sponsored by a family in Manhasset where he played high school lacrosse —the Malloys down on Long island. They were influential with Syracuse University somehow, but they only managed to raise the money for his tuition and expenses. The university put him on the team, but it's my understanding that Jim Brown doesn't have a football scholarship."

Big Mike didn't want to bring up his experience with the country club in Cortland.

"I know what Tall Jerry is saying in his letter is right," Barber said. "The man across from Chubb's bought a television at the state fair and he told my dad that somebody on television was showing news or something about how they won't let some kids go to school in Little Rock with the other kids."

"You mean Jackie and Alda wouldn't be able to go to school in Arkansas?" Mary asked. "I hardly believe that."

"He'd better be careful down there," Mayor said.

"Put the letter away, grab a plate," Big Mike said. "I'll serve in the kitchen and we'll talk while we eat."

Wasn't long before they were in their seats with plates of spaghetti piled high. Two platters sat in the center of the table, one with pan-seared sausage links and one stacked with broiler-toasted, Italian garlic bread.

"We'll call this a supper break," Big Mike said. "If you don't mind, I'd like to get some words in for you to think about. There's more spaghetti and sauce in the kitchen if anyone wants more. Help yourself."

Big Mike twirled his fork in the spaghetti on his plate, looking around at the faces. He'd known the same bright eyes and sincere smiles from the time they were pups. The kids who didn't have a mean bone in their bodies—the same kids who weren't kindly when someone got taken advantage of—were growing up.

He set his fork down.

"When I was a boy, this was back in about 1910, I lived in Minnesota," Big Mike said. "I remember asking my mother why some of the kids I knew lived on reservations. She told me she didn't have an answer—that it was the same way it was in France when she and my dad came to America from Saint-Jean-Port-Joli, Quebec."

"Are you from Canada?" Holbrook asked.

"My parents came to Canada from Normandy."

"In France? You mean like the D-Day Normandy?"

"Yes," Big Mike said. "My parents were French Acadian, and their people were persecuted and sent out of France into Canada. Our name was spelled differently back then.

Most put their forks down and leaned in to listen. Big Mike's stories came with his spaghetti-and-sausage suppers.

"My father died from falling off the barn roof when I was your ages now. Losing my dad was like you and your friends losing people in the war. I was thirteen and quit school and worked wheat fields in the Dakotas to help my mom. That's when I made a decision that I was going to learn about America and learn why some of my friends lived on reservations."

*Big Mike's boyhood home in 1902*

"Is this for real?" Holbrook asked. "You went to the Dakotas alone when you were thirteen?

"That was before cars were invented, right?" Barber asked.

"The point I'm trying to make is that I've seen a lot of things in these states we all call America. I've seen things I'm proud of, and I've seen things I'm not proud of, and I've met a lot of people."

"What was your favorite thing to do?" Randy asked.

"Besides reading books?"

"Yes, sir, your favorite thing you did."

"I'd sit on a mountain ledge in the Black Hills and sing *Home on the Range* and listen to my echo."

"Anything else?" Holbrook asked.

"While I was cooking tonight, I heard Mary read what Jerry wrote. I've seen what he's seeing now in places—and worse."

"Worse?" Mary asked.

"I've never seen one, but there's been lynching. Human beings treated like barnyard animals, disrespected, degraded—even murdered."

Big Mike saw tears glistening in Mary's and Randy's eyes. The others sat in stunned silence. They'd pretty much related that sort of thing to Hitler and the Nazis in the war. This brought it home.

"Why are you crying, Mary?" Barber asked.

"Aunt Lucy…" Mary's voice cracked.

"Is Aunt Lucy…?" Bases started.

Mary looked down with her eyes closed and nodded.

"Two things I'd like to say," Big Mike said. "This is the time, and you're bright, so I'd appreciate you giving them some thought."

"We will," Holbrook said.

Big Mike raised up from the chair and stood every inch of his six-foot-six height. He untied the apron and dropped it on the chair.

"Barber, what am I?" he asked.

"Huh?" Barber asked, completely startled.

"Look at me, son—just tell me what I am."

"Aren't you Big Mike?" Barber asked.

Big Mike looked about.

"What am I?" he asked again.

"Anybody," he said. "What am I?'"

"You're a baker?" Randy asked.

Big Mike raised his arm, swirling his fist in the air.

"Yessss!"

"So, if I'm a baker, then what is Mr. Barber?" he continued.

"A farmer?" Mayor asked.

"How about Mr. Holbrook—what is he?"

"He's a brakeman on the railroad," Holbrook said.

"Now tell me, Mary—you tell me. What is Aunt Lucy?"

"She's a live-in housekeeper. Oh, I get it," Mary said.

"And the Gaines family down the road and left up the hill—what are they? Anybody?"

Murmurs worked themselves about the table.

"Farmers," Holbrook said.

"They're farmers," Randy affirmed.

"Gaines farm—they're farmers," Barber said.

Mary got up from her chair, walked around the table, and gave Big Mike a hug. She whispered "thank you" into his chest.

Mayor spoke up.

"You said there were two things. What's the other thing?"

"Number two is that people are people—the bakers, the brakemen, the farmers, and the housekeepers. They are all people. Skin, race, religion has nothing to do with it. Talk with people—hear them out—learn about their lives, about their customs, about who they are. Give people a chance to be your friend. You can't do all that without becoming friends. Don't make assumptions about who people are because of the way they look. If you have questions about a person's culture or background, break bread with them. We're all one brotherhood and life is too short. The issues Tall Jerry is seeing aren't about anything but people not taking the time to understand other cultures. Sit at their tables, listen and learn. Not at your table—at theirs. They'll be themselves at their table. Don't ever feel so threatened that you'd allow anyone to be caged into categories or into places, like the reservation some of my boyhood friends grew up in."

"What does 'culture' mean?" Holbrook asked.

"Let me explain it in a simple way," Big Mike said.

"Okay."

30

"I'm Roman Catholic. Some of you are Baptists, some are Methodists or other religions. Any of you ever think it's funny the way we Catholics are standing and kneeling during our Masses?"

"It is funny. It'd wear me out going to church there," Mayor said.

"When we get into or out of our pew, we genuflect, or touch one knee to the floor. Want to know why?"

"Tell us," Holbrook said.

"We believe that the church is God's house. We believe He is at the altar. Out of respect for His presence, we always genuflect when we enter or leave His home."

"That's so nice," Mary said.

"How about you, Mayor?" Big Mike asked.

"I understand it now, and it makes sense."

"Now you know a bit of the Catholic culture. Does it help you appreciate our ways better?"

"It does," Mayor said.

"Isn't understanding better than making assumptions without knowing?"

"Yes, sir. It's not so funny after you explain it."

"We need to learn cultures of people instead of laughing at what we don't know," Holbrook said.

Big Mike smiled.

"I'm in the church choir with Jackie and Alda," Mary said.

"The Gaines girls?" Big Mike asked.

"Yes."

"Have you ever shared their table?"

"No."

"Have any of you invited them to join the Pompey Hollow Book Club?" Big Mike asked

"No, sir."

"And they live a stone's throw from here. Is there a reason?"

"Never! No way," Mary said. "None of us think like that—never. They're in different grades in school is all."

"Seventh grade, I think," Randy said. "Alda is a good softball pitcher."

"Come to think of it, the Gaines' place is the only farm in all of the Delphi hamlet that's actually on Pompey Hollow Road—well, at a corner of it anyway," Barber said.

"Mary, let me ask you," Big Mike said. "If Mr. Gaines and Mrs. Gaines are farmers, what are Jackie and Alda?"

Mary didn't hesitate.

"Jackie's a great choir soprano and Alda is the best softball pitcher," Mary said.

Big Mike beamed.

"Atta girl!"

Mary returned an understanding grin.

"Take your plates to the kitchen. Stack them and finish your meeting," Big Mike said. "I'll cut the cake and see you get home if you need rides."

They "got" it—Big Mike's messages about cultures.

They ate cake, and it was a happy time. Mary called the meeting to order again.

"That's all I have," she said through a mouthful of cake. "Write Tall Jerry's address down if you're going to write him a letter. Randy, if you get the secret-code master be sure to tell Barber in case he has to set up another meeting."

"I'll know tomorrow," Randy said.

"Meeting adjourned," Mary said.

Each thanked Big Mike for the evening. They stepped out of the house and off the stoop a little taller, knowing they could make a difference in the world.

The gathering broke up when the Packard drove in to pick Barber and Bases up. Mr. Barber had some night chores that kept him up. He rolled a window down, stuck an arm out, and pointed to Mary.

"How're your folks, young lady?"

"Oh, they're fine."

"Thanks for taking the packages to Aunt Lucy."

"No problem. I'm going there tomorrow after church."

"She's good people, Aunt Lucy is. Gertie met her at a bake sale. We try to help," Mr. Barber said.

Mr. Barber offered Mayor a lift to Penoyer Road, but the lad opted to ride with Randy's pap when he came, so he could pass time jawing with his friends. Holbrook felt the air to see how cold it might be getting. He announced he'd either go with Randy's pap or camp out. He hadn't quite made up his mind.

The Packard rolled down the dirt driveway.

"I'll never understand that whole thing," Mary said.

"What thing?" Big Mike asked through the screen door.

"The Civil War. I thought it ended all that. I don't get it."

No one spoke.

When there are no good answers for a question, silence speaks the loudest.

"I wonder how Tall Jerry's doing?" Mary asked.

"I bet it's warm in Arkansas," Holbrook said.

With a pillowcase filled with provisions over his shoulder, he stepped off the porch, walked down the drive, crossed the bridge, and cut through the alfalfa field to climb the back hill to camp out.

# CHAPTER 6

## MARTY'S GOT THE KEYS

Sunday meetings for the club were a tangle for Mary, as she had morning papers to deliver, early choir practice, and holy services to attend and sing. At two o'clock, Mary had a job today helping clean up after the church social her friend Aunt Lucy was having at her house.

Barber had called the meeting without asking her, which was atypical, and Mary felt a sense of urgency, thinking something might be in the air down in Arkansas. She made a point of being at it. Her dad dropped her off.

As they gathered in the cemetery, Mary looked at her watch.

To get things started, she picked up a pinecone and opened the meeting by pitching it and bouncing it off Mayor's shoulder to get his attention. He was the one who had Barber wake everybody up.

Mayor stood with a look in his eye.

"Marty is supposed to be here," he stuttered.

"He's not here," Mary said.

Mayor stretched his neck, looking down the cemetery's drive. "I hope he gets here."

"Jerry's aunt had her baby," Mary said.

"Who told you?" Barber asked.

"Big Mike called my mom. It's a boy."

"Does that mean Tall Jerry is coming home?" Randy asked.

"I think he has to help some first," Mary said.

"Why does Marty have to be here? Barber asked.

"Did anybody find the code master?" Mary asked.

Mayor chose an effective technique—interruption—to stall.

"I was thinking," he said. "Since Tall Jerry's down in Arkansas, he's traveled more than any of us."

No one responded to the interruption.

"I wonder how many miles that is," Mayor said.

"I went to Binghamton once," Bases said.

"That's in this state," Randy said.

"Well, I went," Bases said.

His point was unclear, even to him.

"Duly noted," Mary said, looking at her watch and shaking her head.

If Mayor had been relying on Marty to carry the meeting, it wasn't looking good for him.

"What's in Arkansas, anyway?" Holbrook asked.

"I only know it's on the Mississippi River," Mayor said. "It's across from Tennessee."

"How do you know so much about it?" Holbrook asked.

"I didn't have a map, so I picked up the telephone and asked Myrtie what she knew about it. She told me a lot," Mayor said.

They heard a horse's hooves trotting as Marty rode up the cinder drive on Sandy.

"Whoa."

Leather creaked as he dismounted, holding a satchel by its strap in one hand and his reins in the other. He dropped the reins, walked toward the group with hat in his hand, and performed the cowboy affectation of wiping his brow with his shirt sleeve. He reached into the satchel and pulled out two wooden cylindrical wheels with small knobs on each end. They were covered with letters and numbers. He held them up.

"Anybody know what these are?" he asked.

No answer.

"Conway and I figured them out in woodshop," Marty said.

"What are they?" Mary asked.

35

"We made them from a picture and a drawing. I'll give you a hint. Somebody famous invented it."

"Pass them around, so we can look," Mary said.

"Where'd you get a picture of it?" Randy asked.

"A teacher took a picture of it at the Smithsonian Museum on the senior class trip to Washington, DC."

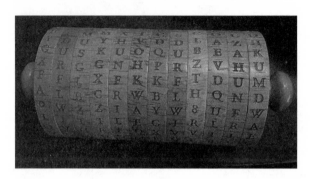

"It looks like a rolling pin for little people," Holbrook said with a grin.

"These are exact replicas of a wheel cipher," Marty explained.

"Wheel cipher?" Mary asked.

"Thomas Jefferson invented it in 1790," Marty said.

"That Thomas Jefferson was a pretty smart, ya know," Randy said.

"It's a wheel what?" Holbrook asked.

"A wheel cipher," Marty said.

"What's it for?" Mary asked.

"Jefferson had to go to France as an ambassador or some big deal," Marty said.

"Was this like after the Revolutionary War?" Mary asked.

"Yes, and he invented this thing so he could pass coded messages to Benjamin Franklin and John Adams without anybody being able to read their secrets and what they were up to. Franklin and Adams went with him to France.

"Why did they have secrets? The French were our friends, right?" Barber asked.

"It was after the French helped us win the Revolutionary War, so there were spies all about. Nobody trusted anybody," Marty said.

"How's it work?" Holbrook asked.

"Pretty simple. Look-see here: It has twelve small, separate wooden wheels attached to it. Try turning them. Each wheel has all the letters of the alphabet jumbled up, and none of the wheels are the same. If you turn the wheels, you can spell a message across any of the lines. After that all you have to do is turn the cipher around and write down a whole other line of letters, any whole line. Send that row of letters as your message. That's the code," Marty said.

"And whoever gets it puts the same line on their wheel and then turn the wheel around until they can read the words you coded?" Holbrook asked.

"And nobody else can decipher the code?" Mary asked.

"Not unless they have one of these, they can't," Marty said.

"And both of these wheel gadgets have the same letters on them?"

"Yup, they're both the same."

"How long did they take you guys to make them in woodshop?" Randy asked. "I only made bookends."

"It took Conway and me a week to make four of them," Marty said. "The wheels are the easy part—you need a jigsaw and a wood drill. We tried to hand carve one letter at a time, but that was going to take forever. I found a set of printer's-type letters from a shut-down newspaper in Tully. We hammered each letter onto a wooden disk on each cipher wheel."

"Get one to Tall Jerry," Mary said.

"Already sent him one," Marty said. "Duba couldn't find the code master, and he called Conway, thinking he had it. Conway came up with the idea to make these, and he called me and suggested we send one to Tall Jerry."

"I'm impressed," Mary said.

"I called Randy, who gave me the address to send it to. I sent it airmail, special delivery," Marty said.

"Tall Jerry should have it any day now," Mayor said.

"The club owes me a dollar forty, and we owe my dad two bucks and ten cents I had to borrow for postage," Marty said.

"It sounds complicated to use," Mary said.

"If Tall Jerry gets in trouble," Marty said. "He'll figure it out quick if he needs it."

"Marty's right," Mayor said. "Who knows what messes Tall Jerry's going to meet up with traveling through all those states? Don't suppose you've read *Huckleberry Finn* and the troubles he gets into. Don't suppose."

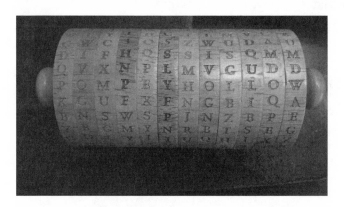

*Mayor sets the cypher wheel to read "Pompey Hollow."*

The code is BNSWSPJNZBPE.

"That makes no sense," Randy said. "Who would Huck send messages to on the river? Jim couldn't read or write."

"Can I have one for a day or so?" Mary asked. "I want to put 'send me a postcard' in code in a letter to Tall Jerry. I collect postcards."

Marty handed a cipher wheel to Mary.

Mary's mind wandered as she examined the wooden mystery, turning its wheels about and aligning up letters. She seemed unsettled and in a daze, like she was wrestling with a matter of some unfinished business.

That was when a chilling breeze through the pine tree startled her. She leaned and picked up the packages Barber had given her to deliver to Aunt Lucy and stood up, holding them with a hug.

"Has Jackie or Alda ever talked to any of you guys about being in the club?" Mary asked.

"What do you think?" Barber said.

"I'm just asking."

"No you aren't," Marty retorted. "You're wondering if there's a reason we didn't ask them into our club."

"I promise I wasn't asking that," Mary said.

"Surprised you'd ask it, then," Marty said.

"Nobody's ever turned away from this club," Barber said.

"Shut up," Mary said.

"Nobody," Holbrook said.

"I didn't mean it the way it sounded," Mary said.

"This Arkansas talk is making us edgy," Marty said.

"Don't worry about it," Holbrook replied.

"You're in the church choir," Mayor said. "Why don't you ask them?"

"Get their number so I can call for meetings," Barber said.

"I think I'll walk over and ask them," Mary said. "Somebody call my dad to pick me up at the Gaines's."

"I'll call when I get home," Randy said.

"What's the best way to get there from here?" Mary asked. "Climb Farmer Parker's hill here and walking down and around that way or walking into the hamlet and over Delphi Falls Road?"

"Into the hamlet and over," Barber said. "I'll walk with you as far as the hamlet."

*The Gaines farm, just up the hill from Maxwell's*

## CHAPTER 7

## MARY SHARES A TABLE

The Gaines farm was sandwiched between Pompey Hollow Road and Delphi Falls Road up the hill from the Maxwell place. Mary walked in the drive and up to the house. There were two barns off to the side. The house was set back under trees.

The side door was open a crack. Mary heard talking inside. She rapped a knuckle on a glass pane. Hearing no response, she edged the door open enough to see people sitting around a kitchen table and a brightly lit bulb on a cord hanging down. Mrs. Gaines, with a skillet of vittles in hand, was restocking a platter on the table. Jackie was reading aloud from a magazine she had rolled to a single page, while most were busy passing food, eating, and listening.

*"Crop fertilizers have become more reliable and predictable, according to Cornell Extension reports. Check with your farm-supply dealer for literature. They will most likely have all the information about their safe use. This winter promises to be productive for farms planting early. Good timing on your seeding and proper fertilization are important, along with the weather, of course."*

Mary decided it best to announce herself before somebody saw her walking in and had heart palpitations.

"Hellooo," Mary cooed.

"Mary! Hi!" Jackie squealed, turning in her seat, standing to greet her choir chum.

"Sorry for popping in like this."

"Not at all, child. Come take a chair and join us," Mr. Gaines said. "You're the Mary girl Alda speaks of."

"I hope she says good things," Mary said.

"We enjoyed all your voices in this morning's services, didn't we, Mae?"

"Such a rainbow of voices," Mrs. Gaines said. "Welcome to our home, young lady."

"They are truly blessed," Mr. Gaines said.

Alda waved at Mary, offering a pretty smile from across the table.

"Thank you, Mrs. Gaines," Mary said, pulling a chair and sitting down.

The lady of the house stood with the heavy skillet in hand.

"Now, Mary, there's no Mrs. Gaines in this house. No Mr. Gaines neither. I'm Mae, and my husband there is Allen. And we're neither a 'Ma' nor 'Pa.' Get that one out of your head, too, if you're thinking of it, and we're definitely not any 'honey this' or 'honey that.'"

She pinch-pouted her lips and squinted with friendly, laughing eyes at the way she was exaggerating the whole name thing.

"Mae and Allen are who we are, and you know the girls."

Mae said her piece and turned toward the cookstove for another load.

"Mae and Allen?" Mary asked. "Well, all right then, with your permission, I can do that."

"That's settled, then," Mae said.

"But my momma would tan my hide if I ever called an adult by their first name, Mrs. Gaines."

"Would you like some puffball, young lady?" Allen asked.

"Puffball?"

"Have you ever had puffball, Mary?" Jackie asked.

"Aren't they the big white balls in the woods we kick and they puff brown powder?"

"That's them," Mr. Gaines said.

"Do you eat them?"

Mae slid a couple of sliced-and-sautéed pieces of puffball onto one side of Mary's plate and scrambled egg on the other side.

"You have to peel the outside off first and then clean the center good before you cook them," Jackie said.

"Momma uses bacon fat to fry them in," Alda said.

"Did you find these in the woods, Jackie?" Mary asked.

"Jackie?" Alda exclaimed.

"What?" Mary asked.

"That girl's afraid of bugs and her own shadow," Alda said.

"I am not," Jackie said.

"Jackie stays here berry-picking, chasing peapods, and calling the cows. She does safe stuff. I'm the one who has to find puffballs," Alda said.

"That's not all true—I like butterflies," Jackie said. "They're insects."

"I chase peapods," Mary said.

"You chase peapods?" Jackie asked.

"You have good bumps around here?" Mary asked.

Country kids in the Crown in 1953 had the household chore of keeping a lookout for bumps in the roads. The harvest trucks would load up with peapods from farms after a day's picking and head for the Apulia Station peapod vinery. If the trucks hit bumps in the road, peapods would bounce off the back. Peapods were on most tables the nights the harvest trucks drove by.

"We have good bumps," Jackie said. "One's on the curve and one behind us on Pompey Hollow Road."

"Only one bump up my way," Mary said. "On Berry Road, but it's a doozy. Lots of peapods fall off."

"Give the puffball a try, Mary. If you don't like it, somebody will," Mr. Parker said.

"I didn't mean to interrupt, walking in like I did, " Mary said.

"You're welcome any time, child," Mrs. Gaines said.

"Jackie, what were you reading when I came in?"

"I read the Cornell Extension farm report to Daddy," Jackie said. "Daddy's a good farmer and likes to stay on top of the latest news. I read about innovative ways to farm and animal diseases—farm news like that."

"Were you finished, or did I—?"

"I was done."

Throughout the depression and the drought, Allen and millions of others in America lived through nomadic times looking for work, hoping to survive a time when some weren't fortunate enough to have an education. Mary surmised from that Mr. Gaines could neither read nor write, which, in that day in time, was no source of embarrassment.

Mary savored a bite of puffball.

"This is good. Kind of like breakfast sausage."

Mrs. Gaines smiled.

"Plenty more."

"Maybe you'll show them a little more respect and not be kicking them when you come upon one in the woods," Mr. Gaines said. He crackled a smile, pleased that Mary was enjoying the experience of their warm table.

*"Plenty more."*

"You're always welcome, Mary, and I mean no disrespect, but was there a reason you dropped by?" Mrs. Gaines asked.

"I had some time before I go to work. I thought I'd come by and see if Jackie and Alda here would like to join our club."

"What club is that, child?"

"Momma," Alda said, "it's the Pompey Hollow Book Club."

"Everybody who's anybody knows about the club," Jackie said.

"Just where'd you learn that sass, girls? Not here in this house, you surely didn't."

"I'm sorry, Momma," Alda said.

"You'll have to pardon me, young ladies. I must not be anybody. Your momma must have been in a library reading a book when the news about the—what did you say the name of the club was again?"

"The Pompey Hollow Book Club, Momma," Jackie said.

"Book club? Our books are in libraries and I take care to get them back on time. I haven't heard of this particular book club."

"It's more of a club where we try to do good," Mary said. "It's not so much about books. We just call it that."

"How can we join, Mary? We're not in your grade," Jackie said. "We're in seventh."

"Our club doesn't care how old anybody is," Mary said.

"Even seventh graders?" Alda asked.

"We started it when we were nine."

"I want to join," Alda said. "Can I, Momma?"

"If it doesn't interrupt chores and schooling—and don't forget we're canning today. Did you girls pick up the cellar like you were told?"

"Yes, Momma."

"I help Momma make jams," Mary said. "It's fun."

"Daddy's a good cook, too," Jackie said.

"Big Mike, Tall Jerry's dad made us spaghetti last night."

Mary looked over at Mr. Gaines.

"What do you like to cook, Mr. Gaines?"

He set his coffee cup down.

"Worked the Pullman from Chicago to New Orleans and back up for nigh on twenty-two years. Never missed a day in all those years. I cooked the meals, breakfast, lunch, and dinner for them who was on board long before I bought this here farm."

"What's a Pullman?" Mary asked.

"What's a Pullman? Why honey, a Pullman is the fanciest train car for passengers there ever was. It has sleeping berths with rich velvets to set on, expensive pillows for resting your head. Why they even have running water. There're lounge cars, too, with bars stocked with the best liquor money can buy and a Pullman dining car as good as the finest New York City restaurants."

"Oh my," Mary said.

"I worked the kitchen in a Pullman dining car for years. I slept between meals on a bunk board in the crew area of the baggage car. I met some nice folks on board, don't ya know. 'Spect I made some friends along the way. Some interesting folks, I surely did."

He picked up his cup and gazed off into the memories.

"Daddy gets Christmas cards from all over the world," Jackie said.

Mrs. Gaines interrupted.

"That's your daddy's business, now isn't it, young lady?"

"I'm sorry, Momma," Jackie said.

"Mary doesn't want to hear such bragging."

"Well it's true, Momma," Alda said. "There's so many we hang them on the Christmas tree after Daddy looks at them."

"Daddy makes the best corned-beef hash in the entire world," Jackie said. "He makes it with the grinder."

She pointed at clamp indentations on the edge of the wooden kitchen table.

"I'm partial to the pickled tongue," Mrs. Gaines said.

"Tongue takes a month, done right," Mr. Gaines said.

"A month?" Mary asked. "So do Mrs. Parker's butter pickles."

"We have a patch of dill in the garden," Alda said.

"Where's your job today, Mary?" Jackie asked.

"Aunt Lucy's place."

"Up by you?"

"She lives up by us."

"Do you like—mow or rake?" Alda asked.

"I wash dishes and help pick up whenever she has a social. She's having people over. These packages are for her."

"Dishwashing is good for the soul," Mr. Gaines chuckled.

"It's because of Aunt Lucy I'm in the choir," Mary said.

"Huh?" Jackie asked.

"I wanted to learn gospel, and I wanted to learn how to sing it well. Aunt Lucy told me the best way to learn was joining your church, because you and Alda were in the choir. She was right."

Jackie beamed.

Mrs. Gaines smiled a kindness Mary's way. "Are the bags linen for the party?" she asked.

"No ma'am. Aunt Lucy collects things—clothing and blankets from the folks she does live-in work for in Syracuse—and she sends them to the poor around Christmas time. She wraps them nice and sends them to the needy. Barber gave these to me to give to her, from Mrs. Barber."

"Bless her," Mrs. Gaines said.

Mrs. Gaines balanced the family's social culture with positive influences, albeit gently, as she knew some attitudes outside of the Crown. She filled her children's world with the busyness of friendly drop-ins, runs to a library, and church gatherings. Mrs. Gaines would take her girls on hikes around the DeRuyter Lake shores to look for arrowheads.

"Aunt Lucy's welcome here. Would you tell her where our farm is?" Mrs. Gaines asked.

"Yes, ma'am. I surely will."

"Bring her by anytime. That would be nice. We'd like to meet her."

"Yes, ma'am."

Mary finished her second breakfast of the day and was about to get up when Jackie handed a basket of bread rolls over to her.

"Daddy brings rolls from a customer in Syracuse—he gets a bagful when he goes on Saturdays to sell eggs and chickens."

"Want to see our room?" Alda asked.

"Sure," Mary said, grabbing a roll.

"Mary," Alda said. "How will I know when you're going to have a club meeting?"

"Barber calls and tells you. Don't worry—if you're out doing chores, he'll keep calling. He's our meeting caller. I need you to write down your telephone number. If you want to come, meet us at the Delphi cemetery at whatever time he says."

Mr. Gaines winced at the thought of the cemetery.

"Well, it'll be quiet—that's for sure," he said, smiling.

*Alda and Jackie, happy Mary dropped in*

Mary's dad honked out front in the drive. She hurried her good-byes and walked out, gnawing on her roll. She had a pleasant feeling about the visit—and about sharing a table.

Mr. Crane dropped her at Aunt Lucy's, who listened intently to her about the Gaines family, about eating puffballs and their house and barn. She couldn't wait to meet them.

"Maybe you can take me there after Thanksgiving, dear," Aunt Lucy said.

"Mrs. Gaines said she would love to meet you, Aunt Lucy."

"After Thanksgiving would be nice."

"My dad will drive you there," Mary said.

"Thanksgiving is the busiest time for a housekeeper."

# CHAPTER 8

## MIDNIGHT IN ARKANSAS

It was late Tuesday night in Little Rock when ole Charlie here's whisper first came to Tall Jerry in the pitch-dark room. First time ever since I died the lad heard my voice. Lying on his stomach, he startled, poked his head up from his cot. He was hearin' my voice, but he didn't know whose it was and wondered what he was hearing in that second-floor where he had to sleep alone.

"Tall Jerry?"

Silence.

"Can you hear me, Tall Jerry?"

Tall Jerry moaned and pulled his blanket over his head. He turned on his cot with a squeaky bounce to face the wall.

"I don't have all night, son. This is ole Charlie."

The room was silent.

"It's almost too late for what I got to tell you, Tall Jerry. You need to get up."

Under the blanket, Jerry's head flinched at every syllable of my voice, like an owl looking at sounds. His head darted up, tightening the knotted-up blanket wrapped over his head like a bridle. This noise sounded like a voice. He was probably thinking he was dreaming.

"Jerry, this is ole Charlie. You got a minute, son?"

Tall Jerry sat up and flipped the blanket off his head, his eyes bigger than Holbrook's peepers the time that dead body came to life up at the Berwyn bathtub. Here he was in Little Rock, alone in the dark and he sees what he thinks is a ghost. He stared straight into a

51

glowing kerosene lantern setting on the floor with my head floating above it– that's right, ole Charlie Pitt's here's head above the lantern and I'm looking him straight in the eye.

"Tall Jerry, it's me."

The lad bolted off the cot like a jack rabbit running from a fox, charged through the ghostly vapor of the lantern glow and my floating head. The boy wanted to leave the room as fast as he could. He grabbed onto the wall and felt his way in the dark to a door and then another door, until he could feel the porcelain bathroom sink in the dark. He looked about to see if the lantern and ole Charlie were still in the room. The lantern was there, glowing like a halo.

Tall Jerry locked the bathroom door, switched the light on and filled the sink bowl with cold water.

He began mumbling to himself.

"What a nightmare," he said. "Holy Cobako! What a danged nightmare." He splashed two handfuls of water into his face and then two more splashes and mumbled some more.

"I wonder why Charlie's in my nightmare," he muttered. "I used to walk the spooky mile to his house in the dark to get the eggs, and I never had nightmares about Charlie like this."

The boy rattled on, cupping more water from the bowl and this time splashing it over his hair. He reached for a towel, put it on his head and stood up to towel off. When he opened his eyes, there I was again, in his bathroom mirror just as clear as the Wizard of Oz. Ole Charlie here was staring back at the lad.

"Yikes!" Jerry yelped, muffling his voice with the towel, so he wouldn't wake anybody downstairs.

"Jerry, calm down. I'm ole Charlie, I just want to talk."

"Bu…bu…bu…but—" Jerry stammered.

"Keep your voice down, son."

"How can you be Charlie?"

"Well, my friend, I'm Charlie, and I'm your guardian angel— have been for a while now."

"Charlie died."

"I'm Charlie, son. If you'll…"

"If you're Charlie, say something only Charlie would know."

"How about I learned you how to free-range chickens, and I gave you a lantern, five wicks, a box of kitchen stick matches, and my hunting knife for Christmas the year I died."

"You are Charlie!"

"It's good to see you, my friend."

"I think I'm going to have a heart attack."

"Let's go to your room, son, where we can talk."

"How come I can see you?"

"I'm your guardian angel, and I wanted you to see me."

"How come I only see your face, Charlie?"

"We do these things in stages. If you'd woken and seen my whole body, you could have had that heart attack you're always going on about, and that would have been just one more thing."

"Are you a ghost, Charlie?"

"I'm your guardian angel. You and all your friends—I'm your guardian angel."

"I knew it!"

"I know you did, son. Thank you for your prayers."

"I knew it all along."

Jerry didn't turn his back on me. He backed into the room to where the cot was. He sat on the edge of the cot while ole Charlie became life-size in my bib overalls and straw hat. I squatted cross-legged on the floor by the glowing lantern as though it were my campfire.

"I think I'm having a heart attack," Jerry said.

"You'll be fine, son."

"Are you real, Charlie?"

"You aren't having a heart attack, and I'm Charlie. Try to calm down."

"Nobody ever told me why you died. Tell me."

"It was the cancer."

"I guessed that, Charlie. It's been, what, four years?"

"I died a considerable time before you put a postcard in that Arkansas mailbox last week."

"You know about my postcard, Charlie?"

"I'm your guardian angel. I know everything. Your postcard is why I'm here."

"Dang, Charlie, if you're a ghost, ghosts are dead people, like zombies."

"Can't be a guardian angel less first you're dead, son—that's a rule."

That loosened Jerry a bit.

"We went to your funeral, Charlie. Mary sang a gospel. She did good but kept crying."

"I know. It was beautiful."

"How'd you become our guardian angel?"

"I knew I was dead when an angel—Arnold—appeared while I was lying there by my back gate."

"Who is Arnold?"

"It works out Arnold was my guardian angel for most of my breathing time on earth—nobody tells you these things when you're alive. He knew my pap. He fought in the Spanish-American War with him under Teddy Roosevelt. They even buried him in Cuba."

"Wait a minute!" Jerry said. "Wait a minute! If all that's true, Charlie, why are you here so I can see you and now you're telling me you're my guardian angel in Little Rock? Am I dead, Charlie?"

"You're not dead."

"Why are you telling me all this? Am I going to die, Charlie?"

"You're not going to die, son—least not yet."

"Why are you here?"

"There's a reason, son. It started earlier this evening when ole Charlie here was setting on my favorite tall pine branch up in your woods at Delphi Falls admiring a glowing full moon."

"You can zip around like that, Charlie?"

"Oh, the lightning was fierce son. Busted a rock loose from the top of the second falls, split my tree."

"That's a thousand miles away from here—maybe more."

"I can, son."

"Are the leaves changing colors back home?"

"Oh my, they're a sparkle, glistening in the autumn frost."

"I'm homesick, Charlie."

"There I be, up tall on my favorite branch. I was in a moment of thought about the Christmas ahead for my flock when I looked up and saw the moon flicker."

"Huh?"

"Yes, sir, the moon flickered. It surely did. It even flickered a full on and off two times."

"You said it was lightning."

"There's still a moon in storms, son."

"The moon doesn't do that, Charlie—flicker. Must have been a cloud covered it."

"Oh, the moon will flicker for an angel, Jerry. It surely will."

"Is that like what they call a miracle or something, Charlie?"

"Oh no, a flickerin' moon can be seen only by guardian angels, and it can mean only one thing, son."

"What's it mean?"

"The angels who can see it are called to a special meet up. Heaven calls these meetups 'angel congresses.' I've been to a few before."

"Holy Moses."

"This meeting will be at the striking of midnight."

"When?"

"Tonight, son."

"Tonight?"

"They take place the night of the flicker and always take place where ole Charlie is, and here is where I am."

"I'm not believing this. It's all a dream."

"Angel congresses mean something's up. It's when we get assignments and questions answered."

"You haven't said where you go for that congress thing?"

"Right here, Jerry."

"Here in my room?"

"It's best we have the angel congress here."

"What!?"

"Here."

"You mean here in Little Rock?"

"Here in this room, son."

"You're kidding, right? I still don't believe…"

"Premonition, son—it's a premonition. I got a sign and I knew you're having issues down here with seeing how some treat other of God's children. Ole Charlie had a premonition I could help you by having you help me with an assignment."

"You promise I'm not going to die, Charlie?"

"I can't promise, son. But you're not dying tonight."

"You know what I mean, here in Arkansas."

"You'll have a long life, Jerry, if you don't go giving yourself that heart attack you keep spouting off about having."

"Charlie, if my mom heard us talking and came up, would she be able to see you?"

"Only you can see me, Jerry. Only you can hear me."

"What do you need from me, Charlie?"

"I'm not certain, son. If we get an assignment we'll have one day before Thanksgiving to do something while you're here in Little Rock. The day after Thanksgiving you and Dick will be heading back to Delphi Falls with Missus."

"I can't wait to get back home. Were you scared coming all this way, Charlie? It's pretty far."

"Perched on a limb, gazing up at the moon over Delphi Falls, I was dreaming of the holidays when I was alive, smells of firewood

TALL JERRY IN HEAVEN SENDS FOR HEMINGWAY

smoke dustin' over the hills. I remembered flaky crusts of apple, pumpkin and mincemeat…that's when I saw the sign."

"I'm sorry you had to die, Charlie."

"That's when the lightning come, and I knew I had to travel here."

"When is this thing again—the meeting?"

"It'll be in this room, in about four minutes."

"Will I be scared, Charlie?"

"No need to be scared. Just sit and listen. We'll talk again after it's over and they've gone."

"They?"

"There will be others."

"Others, you mean ghosts…er…I mean angels?"

"There could be others."

"Who are they? Will I be able to see and hear them?"

"I'm not sure who's coming. We'll see. Only I will be able to see or hear them, son."

"Why? Are they ghosts, too?"

"We like 'spirits,' son. We like 'angels' even better."

"I have to pee."

"Go do your business, son. We still have a little time."

# CHAPTER 9

## NIGHT VISITORS

A voice only ole Charlie here could hear filled the room.

"Who's the young man with you, Charlie?" the voice asked.

"He's one of my flock."

"Charlie, are you talking to me?" Jerry asked.

"No, son, give me a minute."

Tall Jerry jumped back on his cot and bumped his head on the wall.

"It's against the rules for a mortal..." the voice started.

"I know."

"Charlie who are you talking to?" Jerry asked.

"Be patient, son. You can only see and hear me. Sit there and be patient."

"Is there a reason he's here?" the voice asked.

"There is."

"You know the rules, Charlie. Angel congresses are for angels, not for the living."

"I had a premonition."

"Explain your premonition?"

"I conjured it this way, see—I knew this boy was witnessing things the Lord wouldn't find favor with—things the boy had never seen before—being here for the first time."

"And?"

"He's a prayerful lad. I said to myself maybe an angel in this neck of the woods overheard the boy's prayers about what he's been seeing here. I conjured maybe that angel passed an idea on to call an angel congress down here to include him, 'cause Heaven maybe needed help from a mortal somehow. I know how that works at times."

"We know how it works, Charlie," the voice admonished. "Get on with it."

"Well the boy's seeing things down here is when I thought something was brewin' here and the lad might help—you know, something an angel can't do, something only a mortal can do, something important for the Lord. Not that you'd take advantage of the boy's adventuresome nature."

The voice was silent.

"Or of mine."

"Charlie, you're a good shepherd," the voice said.

"Thank ye kindly. I did think it good."

Tall Jerry had a look as if ole Charlie's being there was still a dream, a figment of his imagination and now sounding like he's talking to himself.

"What name does he go by?" the voice asked.

"Jerry."

"What?" Tall Jerry asked.

"Not you son," ole Charlie here reminded the boy.

"Saint Jerome. Impressive. St. Jerome was a librarian. Does he have a middle name?" the voice asked.

"Mark."

"Saint Mark? Another revered..." the voice started.

"It's after Mark Twain, Charlie," Tall Jerry said.

"We understand Jerry belongs to a group who have caught criminals and otherwise unsavory folks. Is this right?"

"Yes."

"We know he has a lot on his mind here in Arkansas ..."

"Are they still talking to you Charlie?" Jerry asked.

"Yes, son. Be still."

"Would the boy like to help us deal with some bad people?"

Ole Charlie here turned to Jerry.

"Jerry, if we need your help down here will you help?"

"I'll help you," Jerry said.

"You can't talk about it, least not until we're finished and gone from here and you're back home at the Delphi Falls."

"I can keep secrets, Charlie."

"Until you're all the way back home, can you do that, Jerry?"

"Who's going to believe I talked to angels?"

"Charlie, the lad's perfect," the voice to Charlie said.

"He's a good boy."

"You did good bringing the congress here."

Jerry sat on the cot with his mouth dropped in awe. He pinched himself to see if he was awake, and sure enough he was. He had seen ole Charlie talk with a voice he couldn't hear.

After a minute of quiet it was like a flashbulb went off, lighting up the room with a blinding flash. Jerry bolted against the wall again when the room went dark again except for the lantern. Rubbing his eyes, he could see through his fists a faint filmy vapor by the wall. Another voice sounded that only ole Charlie here could hear.

"Charlie," I'm William, angel to a flock here in Arkansas, Little Rock, some in southern Little Rock, a few in north Little Rock. I prayed for your ear."

"Why mine, Angel William?"

"Whose Angel William? I see something, Charlie."

"Be still, lad."

"Who are you talking to now, Charlie?" Jerry asked.

Ole Charlie pointed at the cot, indicating that Tall Jerry should sit and just be patient.

"Charlie, do you remember when angel Sir Arthur Conan Doyle appeared to help with that English pickpocket fellow?" angel William asked.

"Oh, he helped me, he surely did. Sir Doyle will be coming back when the pickpocket gets out of jail."

"Charlie, I need help—but from you, this time. I need it for someone in my flock here in Arkansas."

Ole Charlie here was thinking about how we hardly never heard of people in the Crown acting mean to folk up home. Something was trying its best to fit together in my brain. It was all too coincidental, first a voice and now the spirit of an angel being in the room. That's when ole Charlie here took a second look at the angel.

"Might I ask something?"

"Me?" Tall Jerry asked.

"Not you, Jerry."

"Anything, Charlie," Angel William said.

"Son, you can clear the air if you answer me this. Are we here because you've been listening to the prayers of that young man settin' on the cot, and hearing all he's been seeing and feeling here in Little Rock?"

"I won't lie, Charlie."

"You can't lie, son. It's an angel rule."

"What'd he say?" Tall Jerry asked.

"I did hear his prayers, Charlie, and I prayed to see what He could do to get you to help me, like angel Sir Doyle helped you."

"Beggin' your pardon, William, but Sir Arthur Conan Doyle is an expert on a number of things. Ole Charlie here is not much of an expert on anything more than what I know about. Chickens."

"Charlie, we have an idea," the voice said. "Angel William here needs your young man's ear—that's all he's asking. He thinks the lad may be able to help."

"You have our ear, William."

Jerry began to shake. He could only hear ole Charlie here. He grabbed a blanket for balance.

Ole Charlie turned and looked over.

"You may want to listen, son."

"Listen to what? I only hear you."

Angel William's ghostly wave settled as he gathered his thoughts.

"There's a man staying in the Capital Hotel east of here," Angel William started.

"I can hear him, Charlie."

"Just listen, son."

"Charlie, he came to town, went to a church, kneeled and prayed, and then he left and checked into the hotel. He's been checked in the same hotel for two weeks and has never been seen out of his room. He stands by the dresser in his underwear, typing on a typewriter."

"How do you know?"

"I can see him through his hotel room window."

"What's wrong with a man wearing underwear in his room?"

"He didn't check in under his real name."

"I wonder why?"

"He checked in under the name Manolin Santiago."

"Spanish."

"His real name is Ernest Hemingway," Angel William said.

Jerry's heart sank. He knew about Ernest Hemingway. Missus told him she was getting him a Hemingway book for Christmas.

"Why would a man change his name like that?"

"Charlie, the words going around that President Eisenhower is sending army troops down here to Little Rock. Troops to guard children who want to go to school and are being stopped by the governor's office," Angel William said.

"Are you telling me children need troops to walk them to school?"

"In Arkansas, some do, Charlie."

"I can't imagine that."

"The governor has threatened to close all public schools if the president insists on integration."

"Why, the nerve of that b…!"

"Charlie, Hemingway is a famous writer, he's known all over the world. I think he doesn't want folks knowing he's in town peeking about."

"Why not?"

"This man has a nose for smelling stories during times of conflict—even wars," Angel William said. "We know it's Ernest Hemingway."

"Can't say I know the man."

"I know about Hemingway, Charlie," Tall Jerry said.

"Charlie, Hemingway wrote something I found," Angel William said.

"If the man's a man of letters, I'm sure his writing can be found."

"But this is special."

"Why?"

"I'll tell you in a minute."

"How did you get ahold of it?"

"I found it in church some years back," Angel William said.

"Please listen, Charlie," the voice in the room said. "It'll make sense in time."

"Where'd you find it in the church?"

"Under a prayer cushion."

"I said you have our ear and I meant it."

Ole Charlie got on the floor next to the lantern, cross-folded my legs and sat up proper, out of respect.

"Are they gone, Charlie?" Jerry asked.

The ghostly wavy young William vapor backed against the wall to still his image, and unfolded papers. "PH" was scrawled in big letters in black crayon on the front page. He held it up for ole Charlie to see the initials.

# CHAPTER 10

## YOU NEED TO KNOW

"Hemingway wrote books," Angel William began. "Books of wars, of Paris, some of Spain and bullfighting, but there is one about a young Cuban boy named Manolin and the old fisherman, Santiago."

"Where'd I hear those names—Manolin and the other one?"

"From me, Charlie," Angel William said. "Those are the names Hemingway checked in with. He used the name Manolin Santiago."

"Now why would a man do that, use a different name, if he weren't hiding something?"

"His new book is *The Old Man and the Sea,* and it's going all over the world."

"I know about that book, Charlie."

"Hush, son. Just pay attention."

"People will listen if he has something to say, this Hemingway, Charlie."

The young angel stood, catching his thoughts. Ole Charlie pointed to the crayoned "PH" on the paper he was holding up and asked if he knew what it meant.

"The PH? It stands for 'Papa Hemingway.' He was proud when he became a papa. That's why this piece of paper is special."

The young angel looked at the floor with somber eyes.

"Hemingway wrote this story about a lady having a baby in 1937. How her youngest son had to run find the doctor late at night and how the baby girl was a blessed baby," angel William said.

"Women have babies all the time, William."

"This baby's name was Anna Kristina. Mr. Hemingway wrote about the night baby girl, Anna Kristina, was born," angel William said.

The voice spoke.

"We think Ernest Hemingway is in Little Rock to write about the school children who aren't being let into public schools. We believe finding these papers in that church was a sign of trouble."

Through the vapor a worried look could be seen in William's eyes, filling with tears, as though he wasn't the one who needed help.

"I'm thinkin' you know this baby girl, William. The baby girl Anna Kristina, in the story."

"I do, Charlie."

"How do you know her, son?"

"Anna Kristina was my sister."

"You're the youngster who fetched a doc when she was born?"

"Yes."

"Where was your pap when this was happenin'?"

"Pa went to Louisiana for bait-shrimp work before Momma had the baby, but he never came back."

"Never?"

"He never saw the child."

"What is your momma's name, son?"

"Daisy Pearl, but I called her 'Momma.'"

"And this Daisy Pearl—your momma, son—where is she now?"

"We lost momma when Anna Kristina was four."

"Not a well woman, was she?"

"Charlie, I was a mess-cook helper in the navy in 1941. I lied about my age and joined—thought I could see the world in the navy."

"How old were you, son?"

"Almost seventeen."

"That's young for navy duty, son."

"I was killed in the Pearl Harbor attack, Charlie."

"That could crush a mother's soul."

"My dying is what put Momma down, Charlie."

65

"I can understand that."

"Her dying made Anna Kristina's life a struggle, having to survive best she could."

"How'd she fare, son?"

"She was orphaned and went into foster homes."

"Orphaned at four? Wasn't there any family to help her?"

"I have a brother, Aaron."

"Where was Aaron?"

"Brother Aaron couldn't deal with the losses, mine and Momma's. He joined the army air corps right after Momma died. It was too much for him. He didn't wait for the draft. They kept him busy, taught him a lot—all about planes and how to fly bombers—so that was good."

"Like to fly, did he?"

"He was a good pilot, but he never had a chance overseas."

"Was he needed here at home, son?"

"Charlie, some in the air corps in World War II were kept on the ground, working on planes. Oh, the boys from Maxwell and Tuskegee went, but they didn't see action unless they were in fighter planes, Red Tails."

"Where is all of this going, son?"

"Charlie, I'm Anna Kristina's guardian angel."

"Good choice."

"Aaron lives in North Little Rock Charlie," Angel William said. "He doesn't talk much. Since the war, he's not been himself."

"Is there a reason?"

"They broke him, I think, giving him all that training flying airplanes, big important ones, and never sending him or his troop over for action."

"Not any?"

"Not one. That made him feel lesser than the man our momma told us we were."

"That could be demoralizing, son."

"Momma would tell us to stand straight and tall, and she would say we could do anything and be anybody if we kept looking up. That's why Aaron joined the air corps after she and I died. He wanted to show her he was a man."

"Taking care of his sister would have done that, son."

Jerry could tell by the look in ole Charlie here's eye something was brewing.

"One of them, your sister Kristina or your brother Aaron, is in trouble, right?"

"Yes, Charlie."

"Which one, son? What trouble?"

"Kristina's pregnant, Charlie."

"The girl can count on ole Charlie here for prayers."

"She's sixteen and pregnant."

"Oh my."

"What happened, Charlie?" Jerry asked.

"A sixteen-year-old girl is pregnant, son."

The voice spoke.

"The father is twenty-two, Charlie and with her only being sixteen, it's statutory."

Ole Charlie here slumped in a misery and thought through all I heard. I stood up in a bolt.

"William, I'm not an educated man, but I'm smart enough to know there's somethin' you're not telling me. I'd appreciate your stop slinking around like an alley cat. A girl's alone somewhere—maybe in harm's way while we're here blabbering."

"She is," Angel William said.

"And the girl holds favor with the Lord, or else this Hemingway fellow wouldn't have written about her and we wouldn't be here talking about it."

"Charlie, the baby's father is not a nice person," Angel William said.

"Did the lad hurt her, son?"

"He made his way with her, but they're in love. He didn't physically hurt her. She was willing, but being that he's in his twenties, and she's sixteen, the age difference breaks the law."

"What'd he say, Charlie?" Jerry asked.

"Be quiet son."

"Does the man care about the girl? Does she have feelings for him?"

The voice filled the room.

"Charlie, they care for each other but the lad's been steering her heart with wrong intentions for a time, but he's not our problem."

"Tell me everything."

"It's his father who's the problem," the voice said.

"What about his pap?"

"His father works for the governor in the state capital. If that man ever finds out about this girl…well… he's been known to burn crosses and has a short tolerance for some folks, and he declares it in the open in public. He's not letting some children go to public schools. If this man-demon ever finds out that an innocent girl like Anna Kristina is having his grandbaby, that baby won't stand a chance of seeing the light of day."

"How far would he go?"

The voice didn't respond.

"He'd go that far, Charlie," angel William said.

"Is she along?"

"Eight months."

Ole Charlie circled around the room, muttering to myself.

"So, tonight's meeting was arranged by heaven."

"It was, Charlie," the voice said.

"Until tonight, I didn't know where Arkansas was, but I do know we're here flappin' our gums when there's work to be done."

"That's why I'm here," angel William said.

"By the way, what's this Hemingway fella got to do with this, anyway? Why's he here again?"

"All we know is he's hereabouts for some reason, Charlie. We don't know why. We know he likes bullfights and he jumps in the middle of fights and writes about them when he's not throwing a fist at the devil. Like I told you, we think Hemingway heard President Eisenhower might send troops here. Hemingway must smell a story, or why else would he be holed up in a hotel room?"

"Does he know about this—about the girl and her carrying a baby and all?"

"No," Angel William said.

"How do you know he's not like the others down here?"

"Hemingway's a citizen of the world, Charlie," Angel William said. "His fight is for anyone's freedom."

"Tell me the bigger picture."

The voice spoke.

"We think his story about Kristina, might stir his conscience again. Stir it enough to make him want to help."

"You mean if he reads it, he will help?"

"Yes."

"If who reads it, Charlie?"

"Hemingway son, be still."

"If the man wrote it, he's already read it, I would reckon."

"He wrote the story sixteen years ago. He could have forgotten it by now. If he reads it again and then hears the story of the fix she's in now, he might want to help."

"Charlie, can I say something?" Tall Jerry asked.

"Go ahead, son."

"If what I hear is right Ernest Hemingway wrote a story that will remind him about a girl who's in trouble and if he read it again so that he remembered things, and somebody told him about the trouble she's in, he might want to help, right?" Tall Jerry asked.

"We just said that."

"Well I couldn't hear whoever you're talking to," Tall Jerry said.

"What's your point, son?"

"My point is he likes kids. That's why he calls himself Papa Hemingway. My mom told me that…and that's why he'll see me."

"Does he have an idea, Charlie?" Angel William asked.

"Charlie, I know he wrote a book, *The Old Man and the Sea*. It's about an old man and a young boy. Hemingway respects kids. Give me that paper and I'll take it to him tomorrow and get him to read it, and then I'll tell him about the girl and the trouble she's in."

"You'd do that, son?"

"Just tell me where the hotel is. I'll do it."

"Now I know why we're here."

"The girl, Kristina?" Jerry asked.

The voice spoke.

"Her baby isn't in a flock at all until birth. A womb is in God's kingdom. Angel rules change in order to care for them—unborn babies. That's why we've chosen Jerry, to help, and that's why he can see you Charlie, his guardian angel."

"What's he saying?" Jerry asked, pointing at the wall.

Ole Charlie here looked over at Tall Jerry.

"Jerry, we prayed it would be in your nature to help, but it was up to you to make the decision on your own. Otherwise this all would have been just a dream for you."

"Just tell me what you need me to do, Charlie."

"How will you manage to get out of the house alone, son?"

"Not sure yet."

"I won't be able to go with you."

"I'll think of something to tell my mom, like I'm taking a bus ride, going to the zoo or something. I won't lie, I'll get off the bus at the zoo and walk from there to the hotel where Ernest Hemingway is. I'll walk the whole way."

Angel William smiled. His prayer had been answered. His vapor disappeared into the night and the paper in his hand floated down and rested on the floor.

Just as ole Charlie here was about to talk, there came a knock on Tall Jerry's door.

After the second knock, there came a loud whisper from the hall.

"Jerry?" Missus asked. "Is someone in there with you?"

## CHAPTER 11

## TALL JERRY'S WAKE-UP CALL

When Tall Jerry opened the door, his mom was standing there.
"Who are you talking to, son?"

"Nobody, Mom."

"I heard you talking."

Missus had come upstairs because she'd heard Jerry talking. The lad knew she couldn't hear ole Charlie here, so he convinced her he'd been sleepwalking, having a dream, and talking out loud in his sleep. She was okay with that. She poured him a glass of water and put him back to bed, asking him why he had left the bathroom sink running.

"Oh, that," he told her. "It was the weirdest dream."

She believed him and let it be.

Jerry barely slept all night.

That morning, Wednesday before Thanksgiving, Jerry folded the "PH" papers Angel William had dropped, stuffed them into his jean's back pocket, and went down the back stairs to Aunt Mary's first-floor apartment. He paused outside, his hand on the doorknob. He stood, thinking how his life had changed the night before. He would never be the same. He wasn't sure of the rules for meeting angels, but he knew that until he got home to Delphi Falls he had to keep it all a secret. He also knew folks were depending on him. He took a deep breath, exhaled, and opened the door.

"Drink your juice," Missus said. "Dick and Jerry, see to it that Tommy, Timmy, and Teddy drink their juice." (Aunt Mary's sons.)

"When is Aunt Mary coming home?" Jerry asked.

72

"Tomorrow, dear," Missus said. "She had the baby Sunday and they hold mothers for five days to make sure things are normal. She'll be home for Thanksgiving tomorrow."

"When are we going back to Delphi Falls?"

"On Friday, son. Eat your oatmeal. We leave Friday morning."

Tall Jerry knew he had no time to spare.

"Dick, where are the maps you and Mom used to get here?"

"They're in the glove compartment," Dick said.

"Is there, like, a city map of Little Rock in there, too?"

"No, but Don has a city map on his desk. What's up?"

"I need you to show me something on it after breakfast."

"What do you want to know?"

"A place."

"What place?"

"Can't you just show me without a lot of questions?"

"Why're you being snappy?"

Missus remembered Tall Jerry's "nightmare."

"Dick, show him the map and answer his questions. Be a good brother."

Jerry appreciated his mom's sticking up for him.

Then she went and ruined it all.

"What do you need to know about a Little Rock map, Jerry?" she asked.

"I'm going for a walk."

"Where to?" Dick asked.

"I'm just going for a walk, and I don't want to get lost."

"Where you going?"

" I don't know what the big deal is."

"Dick, show Jerry the map and help him," Missus said.

After breakfast, Dick and Jerry went to the secretary's desk and unfolded the city map. Jerry pulled his sleeve up and looked at the scribbling he had written on his forearm with ballpoint pen.

"Where are we on it?"

Dick pointed to a spot. "Here's where we are."

"I'm looking for West Markham and Main," Jerry said.

"What's at West Markham and Main?" Dick asked.

Jerry poked Dick in the ribs, giving him that *just shut up and help me, I'll tell you later* look.

Dick handed Jerry a blank envelope from the desk.

"Write this down," he said.

Jerry pulled the hassock over to the chair Dick was sitting on and sat, using his knee as a writing surface.

"You walk on Battery for three blocks to Wright Avenue."

"Which way?"

"What do you mean?"

"Do I go left on Battery or right?"

"You go out the door and go left."

"Okay."

"Left on Battery, three blocks to Wright Avenue."

"Got it."

"Go right and walk for—hang on. One, two, three, four, five, six. You go for seven blocks to South Chester Street.

"Seven blocks to South Chester Street."

"You walk thirteen blocks up to West Third Street."

"Which way?"

Dick pointed to the map.

"Look here—go this way."

"Okay."

"You walk eight or ten blocks, and you'll be here."

Dick pointed to the spot on the map.

"Thanks," Jerry said.

Jerry folded the envelope and stuck it in his pocket. Dick followed him out to the porch.

"What's up?" Dick asked.

"I just want to go for a walk, is all. I have two rolls of 127 film left and I want to take some pictures."

"Yeah, right."

Dick wasn't buying it. He knew something was fishy, but he knew Jerry, and he knew he was stubborn. Jerry would tell him when the time was right.

Each step Jerry took was intimidating. He found himself muttering questions to ole Charlie, hoping I'd appear and walk with him. He watched city buses drive by and smelled their diesel fumes. He saw ladies in starched maid's uniforms getting off buses at corners and walking to driveways and up to the side or back doors of houses. He could hear a radio through an open window of a brick house. Some lady was singing inside.

The hotel was big, with beautiful red awnings. It seemed to fill the city block like the Hotel Syracuse, the hotel he worked at that summer. A granite sign on its corner said that Ulysses S. Grant stayed there. As he stepped into the lobby, a doorman in a velvet coat and a top hat started.

"May I help you, sir?"

"No, thanks. I'm meeting somebody," Jerry reported.

"Very good, sir."

In the lobby was a man on a tall ladder decorating a pine tree for Christmas. The ceiling was a stained-glass design that let in light from the roof many floors up. Jerry walked slowly, taking everything in while he looked for elevators. Seeing one, he went to it and stepped in.

"Floor, please?"

Jerry pulled his shirtsleeve up to the ballpoint pen markings on his forearm.

"Third floor, please."

"Very good, sir."

*Capital Hotel Christmas tree.*

Jerry stepped off the elevator and looked at the sign telling him that room 305 was to the right.

"I'm going to have a heart attack…" Jerry said to himself. "Like it could happen at any moment."

He went to the door with 305 on it, stood there and gulped.

He knocked.

No answer.

He knocked again.

"Go away!" a voice inside said.

Tall Jerry knocked again.

The door swung open with a heave. There the man was, tall and wearing baggy pants and a wrinkled sweater. His hair and white beard were dripping wet, as if he had just splashed his face and head to wake himself up. Looking practically eye to eye with Jerry, he stepped back.

"Who are you, and what do you want?"

"I have a delivery for you."

"There are no deliveries for me."

"What do you mean?"

"I'm not here. Go away."

He started to push the door closed. Jerry stuck his foot in the jam, blocking it.

"I know who you are. I'm supposed to make a delivery."

Hemingway paused, stood tall, and cocked his head with a smirk.

"Just who am I, son?"

"You're Mr. Santiago," Jerry said.

Hemingway harrumphed and started to push on the door to close it.

"Some other time, young man," he growled.

"Wait. I know who you are."

Jerry looked up and down the empty hallway.

"You're Ernest Hemingway."

Hemingway bolted.

"I promise, Mr. Hemingway, I have something important for you. Please let me in."

He pulled the door open.

"You're a deceptive young pissant, son. Come in and say your piece."

"Thank you."

"Tell me who the bastard was who told you I was here before I throw you out a window."

Tall as he was, Tall Jerry was trembling head to foot. It wasn't that he was afraid of Hemingway. He was afraid he would say the wrong thing to this man who the entire world knew.

"Mr. Hemingway, I have some papers here. It's important that you read them out loud while I'm here."

"What's this all about?"

"Read them and then I'll go, if you want me to. I'll keep the secret that you're here. I promise."

"You're a writer, son."

"What?"

"You want me to read something you've written so you can tell your friends Hemingway read your work. I get it."

He turned and lifted a bottle of scotch from his bedside table.

"You wrote this, Mr. Hemingway."

Hemingway looked around at Jerry with the bottle's cork in his teeth.

"What in hell?" He spit the cork out.

"You wrote it, sir—honest."

Jerry pulled the papers from his pocket and unfolded them.

"Let me see."

"Only if you promise to read it out loud."

"You're trying my patience, kid."

"You have to read it."

"You like to fight?"

"You have to promise."

"You've already read it, son. Give it here, and I'll know if it's mine."

"I haven't read it, Mr. Hemingway, but it's yours. I know it is."

"If it's mine, where'd you get it?"

"I can't tell you that."

"Can't? Or won't?"

"If I told the truth you wouldn't believe me, Mr. Hemingway, and you like the truth."

"You've been reading my press, kid."

"It would be the truth, but you wouldn't believe me."

Hemingway tipped and finished a jigger of scotch.

"You've been reading too much O. Henry, kid."

"Promise!"

"You run a hard bargain. Give me the papers."

"Thank you."

Jerry handed him the papers, Hemingway looked at him with a wrinkled brow.

"You ever thought of bullfighting, son?"

Jerry's mind raced to an image of Barber's grumpy, ringed-nose bull.

"No, sir."

"Sit on that bed. You want a juice or something?"

"No thank you."

Hemingway sat on the other, opened the paper and scanned a page.

"I'll be goddamned," he said.

"Are you going to read it, Mr. Hemingway?"

He looked at another page.

"I'll be goddamned," he said.

*"I'll be goddamned."*

# CHAPTER 12

## HEMINGWAY READS

Hemingway looked over at Jerry with an inquisitive look. For the first time, Hemingway accepted there was more to Jerry than a stack of paper. He placed the sheets beside him on the bed and picked up one page at a time.

"Keep your mouth shut, kid. Listen."

Jerry nodded.

Hemingway cleared his throat with two cigar cough hacks and began reading.

*Daisy Pearl was named after a slave her mother admired. She was in her late forties the night her water broke and she cramped over, slumping against a wall by the cast-iron Franklin cook stove.*

*It might have been heat that took her into early labor, but some thought she was too old. Her shoulder felt the burn of the wall as bursitis pain ripped through her worse than the cramps, causing a wail that could be heard in the still-night Arkansas air clear past the tracks, and those were two shanties away.*

*William heard the scream and took off running barefoot through lightning bugs for the doc's place in the vicinity of the Sears. Doctor Jefferson didn't live near the tracks, but this was 1937, and she was the only doctor there was in the area, and she kept a lantern lit signaling "Welcome" for this sort of medical inconvenience. Day or night made her no never mind she would remind folks.*

*The head came out and touched the kitchen table more than three months early and in candlelight. The little mite was shy of four pounds—Doctor Jefferson surmised that by cradling the baby up in the palms of her hands, which reflected the glisten of the walking lantern over next to her open bag on the ledge of the sink. Baby wasn't bigger than the doc's two hands end to end.*

*"She's not breathing, and I can't find a pulse," the doc said.*

*With Daisy Pearl lying back, her head leaning off the chipped porcelain tabletop, Doctor Jefferson tried what she knew but pronounced the baby dead.*

*The doc cut the cord to Daisy Pearl's favor, wrapping the balance around the baby, while an emptiness shared about the night, riding on shadows like waves with no names roll to shore the way they do. A little one didn't stand a prayer birthing this early in term, and she was meant to come and leave alone, dead. Daisy Pearl leaned up on her elbows, paused, and pursed her lips, staring off into a lonely dark, avoiding looking down at her baby. She thought of her own momma being born in a cotton field and of her grandmother having to keep picking the cotton until sundown, stopping only to nurse.*

*This happened fast for Daisy Pearl.*

*She stepped from the tabletop, turned in the dark, and rolled the lifeless body and the cord in a section of the blood-spotted morning newspaper she had been lying on. She lifted the lid of the firewood bin and put the package on some kindling at the left end of it but paused, and she asked William to hold the lid up for her. She disappeared into the next room and returned muttering gentle little-girl words in prayer for her lifeless doll, and she carefully folded a hand-stitched baby blanket, lifted it to her face, and smelled it and kissed it a final good-bye. Resting it on top of her dead baby, she slowly lowered the lid.*

*"Pastor Wright will say proper blessings and handle the matter of my baby girl with the Lord tomorrow," she whispered in the dark, trying to convince herself she'd be fine. "First light, William, see to it you pass the word."*

*"Yes, Momma," William told her.*

*"And be sure to tell Pastor Wright my baby's name. Let him know it's Anna Kristina."*

*"Yes, Momma."*

*"Anna Kristina is your baby sister's name," Daisy Pearl said. "Don't you ever forget that name, William."*

*"God bless you, Daisy Pearl," the doctor said as she closed her bag with a snap and lifted the walking lantern.*

*"Sister, you get some rest. You're momma enough as it is already with two fine grown boys. This wasn't to be is all. Promise me you'll get some rest."*

*Doctor Jefferson pushed on the screen door and left for home, and she didn't ask for money, and she didn't let the screen door slam.*

*It was two the next morning when William's brother, Aaron, came home from working at the railroad depot. The train yard foreman fetched him the day before to help stack boxes and shipping crates for a dollar, if he didn't mind earning slave wages. He put the two fifty-cent pieces on the table for his momma. He felt around the table and picked up the candle, lit it, reached over, and lifted the lid off the stockpot filled with bouillon simmering a gristly soup bone. He set the lid back down and leaned over to open the icebox, looking for food like anyone would do after a hard night of sweat and toil.*

*Other than the shadows of a couple of eggs and bacon lard, the shelves were as barren as the night and just the same as he'd found them before he'd gone off to work. He closed it and settled for a can of salmon from the cupboard. He pitched it into his mouth with the fork he'd gotten from the sink. About the time he dropped the empty can in a trash bucket, he felt air from a window crack, and decided to stoke the cookstove for his momma's stockpot before going to bed.*

*He stepped over and lifted the lid of the woodbin. He noticed the baby blanket she had been stitching on for some time now. He reached back for the candle and pulled the blanket out. His eyes caught the rolled-up newspaper on the stack of wood, and he picked it up in his big right hand. He turned the package about to feel what might be in it, and the bloody water seeped out and dripped red over his hand and shirt sleeve. He bolted back in fear, quickly dropping it and the lit candle to the floor.*

*That baby started crying from inside that package on the floor—that's what my notes say. Oh my, how she did cry, they say, and she was alive and saved.*

*Anna Kristina was reborn on the morning after she first came into the world.*

"It's a miracle," Doctor Jefferson said.

"Praise Jesus," Daisy Pearl rejoiced.

*The woman gently lifted her left breast, pressing the nipple near to the baby's face, while her outstretched little finger tenderly touched the newborn's gums and lips to stimulate her suckling instinct.*

"This baby has two birth dates," Doctor Jefferson said.

"Praise the Lord," Daisy Pearl said.

"The cord I left on her and the warmth of the newspaper inside that woodbin must have acted like an incubator, and the shock of the fall to the floor jarred her little lungs awake."

84

Hemingway stopped reading, looking over the last page like a fond old memory—a friend he remembered sweating over and had probably misplaced in some forgotten tavern under a whisky glass.

Jerry was wiping tears with his sleeve. Tears not about the story but the trouble he knew the same girl was in. He felt like he knew her personally.

"Can I say something, Mr. Hemingway?"

He looked over at Jerry, giving the lad a feeling the man was looking at him differently, like it was important to his life that Jerry had come.

"Did you write it, Mr. Hemingway?"

"You know I did. It's true, and it's alive."

He looked at Jerry with a wince.

"What is your name, kid?"

"Jerry."

He extended his hand.

"I'm Ernest, Jerry. My friends call me Ernest or Papa."

"Thank you, Ernest. My friends call me Tall Jerry."

"Talk to me, Tall Jerry. Speak with honest sentences."

"I'm thinking you must have known this baby girl—the one in the story," Jerry said.

"I knew the doctor."

"Oh? The one in the story?"

"Don't waste breath on stupid questions, Tall Jerry."

"How did you know her?"

"We met at a Red Cross relief station before the war. She was giving tetanus shots to civilians. She told me the story and it made an impression on me. I remember. First woman I think I loved. I wrote it to give it to her as a thank-you for putting up with my bullshit at a bar. Leaving the bottle of bourbon for my writing it and taking off was her idea, not mine. I never saw her again."

"Well the lady you wrote about who had the baby, the Daisy Pearl lady, died after her son was killed at Pearl Harbor," Jerry said.

"Aaron was killed?" Hemingway asked.

"William," Jerry said. "Her youngest son. He was sixteen. He lied about his age and joined the navy. He was seventeen when he died."

Hemingway was experienced with war and dying all over the world. Battle casualty meant something to him.

"He died bravely. He died for his country. We owe him," he said. "Why are you here, Tall Jerry?"

"Anna Kristina."

"Anna Kristina in trouble, is she?"

"She's pregnant, sixteen and pregnant, Mr. Hemingway."

Hemingway gazed at Jerry for more.

"They think it's an older guy, like in his twenties, so that would be bad, right?"

Hemingway stood and yelled, "What!"

He grabbed a pillow, swung it around and threw it against the bedside lamp, tearing the lampshade and knocking it over.

"What kind of bastard would do—"

"They said he didn't force himself on her, and he didn't hurt her, but he's in his twenties, and she's just sixteen. That's bad, right?"

"How old are you, Tall Jerry?

"Twelve."

Hemingway looked at Jerry's height.

"You're an old twelve, my friend."

"We grew up in the war, Mr. Hemingway. We were old at six."

Hemingway plopped on the bed, his shoulders slumped.

"Say what they may, I believe in God, and I pray. I've never judged a man by his skin or his creed. I take issue with any coward who does. That's why I'm here, dammit. I don't know how this journey of yours started, but it was heaven-sent."

"You can say that again," Jerry said.

"Tell me everything, Tall Jerry. Tell me why you came here."

Ernest Hemingway sat and listened to Jerry, a kid from Delphi Falls, and a story about a girl in trouble and the man in his twenties' father.

"His father works for the governor. If he finds out…well…I mean, they say he burns crosses and hates some people and says it right in public. He won't let some kids go to public schools. Anna Kristina's baby may not stand a chance if he ever finds out it's his son's baby."

"I've seen his slime before."

"So, you don't know where the girl is, Mr. Hemingway?"

"It's been sixteen years, Tall Jerry. That's a long time. There's been a world war and a lifetime thrown in between."

"Oh."

"Is that why you came? To see if I could help?"

"Yes."

Hemingway stood.

"Get me names; get me the son of a bitch's old man's name. Let's catch that SOB."

"I'll do my best."

"Get me something more to go on, Tall Jerry."

"So, here's the deal, Mr. Hemingway."

"Ernest or Papa, dammit!"

"So, here's the deal, Papa. I'll try to get information today and tomorrow, but I have to leave Friday. If I find stuff after we leave, I won't know how to mail it to you if nobody knows you're here."

"Where are you going?"

"Mom, my brother and I have to go home—the Delphi Falls in New York State."

"If you live way up in New York, how did you wind up in this mess here in Little Rock?"

"You live in Cuba and you're here."

"I'm Ernest Hemingway, Tall Jerry. I live everywhere."

"Stop fooling around. Tell me how I get messages to you."

"Ernest Hemingway, this hotel. I'll tell the desk."

"Okay, good."

"Can you come back later or tomorrow?"

"Why?"

"I'll address and stamp postcards for you. Write messages on the postcards and drop them in the mail."

"How long will you be staying here?" Jerry asked.

"I'll be here until I leave. After that I'll go to Cuba to drink and catch marlin or Africa to drink and hunt, but they'll forward my mail."

"Thank you, Papa. You won't regret this. I promise."

"How are you involved with all of this, Tall Jerry?"

"I'll tell you what I know if we save this girl. I promise. Right now, I can't."

"Be a writer, kid. You're observant, and you have a soul."

Ernest Hemingway shook Jerry's hand, stepped into the hall to watch him walk the hall and around the corner to the elevator.

*Don ready to fly a B-17 to England in 1944*

## CHAPTER 13

## DON CARVES AND JERRY READS

On Thanksgiving morning Missus told Jerry not to wander off. She might need him to do something. There weren't any kids outside like the weekdays he'd been there. Most of the kids must be sleeping in because of the holiday or in kitchens, smelling pies and bread stuffing. Jerry had to figure a way to get back to the hotel to get Hemingway's postcards before they left.

Battery Street in front of Aunt Mary's apartment duplex had a one-block strip near Twenty-First. There was a boulevard of lawn down its middle. Jerry sat alone in the center of it, his mind bouncing like a ping-pong ball between thoughts of friends back in Delphi Falls and meeting ole Charlie. He wondered if he was hallucinating the whole thing, if he was touched in the head. Then there was Ernest Hemingway. Jerry knew he was real, but he knew nobody would believe he'd met him.

He looked around to see if anyone was watching.

"Charlie, are you here?"

He waited.

"Charlie?"

He gave him a minute.

"Charlie, will I ever see you again?"

No response.

He was all alone. With so much to think about and nobody to talk, Jerry felt the Arkansas heat. He was disappointed that he hadn't had a sit-down with his hero, Don, for the stories he'd promised about the war and flying B-17 bombers. Between his job and having to visit the hospital, he'd come home late, sleep and get up early, shave and leave for work.

Jerry went inside, but Missus ordered him out of the kitchen if he was going to mope around and keep sticking his finger in the butter sauce for the fruitcake. She had a turkey to baste and rolls to bake, all while she had to keep the green-bean-and-onion-crisp casserole from burning.

"Go outside and play," Missus said.

"With who?" Jerry asked, pleading his case.

"With 'whom,' dear. Go out and play with whom."

His head sank. Missus rethought her command, understanding it was a holiday. Dick was washing, scrubbing pots and pans.

She waved the turkey baster like John Phillip Sousa's baton, pointed toward the door, and suggested Jerry go wait outside for Don to come home with aunt Mary and the new baby.

"They'll be here any time now."

Don was his hero.

"Just don't go wandering off."

"I won't."

"When they get here, be a gentleman and carry Aunt Mary's bag."

The green '49 Oldsmobile, drove up and pulled by the curb. Don jumped out with a grin, skipped around and opened the door for Aunt Mary, who was holding a new baby son, wrapped in a swaddling blanket. Jerry opened the rear door, grabbed her bag and followed them into the house.

Don stood guard over the turkey. He got his carving set, raised the deer-horn handled knife in one hand, the sharpening steel in the other, and sharpened the blade with a few slither-swipes up and down.

"Please take a seat," Missus said. "Jerry, you sit next to Don."

"There's something on my chair," Jerry said.

"It's mail for you."

"Did they come today?"

"Yesterday."

"These could be important, Mom."

"Put your napkin on your lap."

Jerry ripped open a package from Marty and held the cipher wheel, turning it about, staring at it. He handed it to Don while he looked at a postcard and two letters. The postcard from Mary was in code, one letter from Mayor, and one from his dad.

Don set the cipher wheel on the table in front of Jerry's plate and picked up his carving knife.

"It looks like it's for codes," he said.

"It is?" Jerry beamed.

Don finished carving the turkey.

"Missus, will you do the honors?" Don asked.

"Lord, we thank you for this precious baby and for his young brothers who can watch over him. Thank you for this food and for our loving get-together, and please watch over Big Mike and give us safe passage tomorrow as we start our journey home. Amen."

"Thank you for coming. You were great help for us," Aunt Mary said. "I know Dick and Jerry missed Thanksgiving parties and dances to come here. Thank you."

"Want me to read Dad's letter?" Jerry asked.

"Of course, dear, but quickly, before the food gets cold—and elbows off the table."

"I'll serve the turkey," Don said. "Pass your plates."

Jerry tore the envelope.

"*Jerry, me boy!*"

He looked up at Don.

"Dad calls me that."

*Have fun in Little Rock and take lots of pictures of your adventures. Invite Don and Mary to bring the kids to Delphi Falls for Christmas and New Year. Santa will come here. See you all when you get home Sunday. Love, Dad.*"

Jerry looked at Don. "Will you come?"

He was busy serving.

"I'd love to see the falls again," Aunt Mary said.

"Can you come, Don?" Jerry asked.

"Don, you have vacation time and the babies travel well."

"We'll let you know soon, if that's okay," Don said.

Missus smiled her approval.

"Grownups, pick up a serving dish or bowl, take for yourself and some for a little one beside you, and pass it on," Missus said.

"Small portions on the little ones' plates, please," Aunt Mary said.

With the laughter and festivities going on at the table, Jerry's mind wandered, and he thought about meeting ole Charlie here and if he'd ever see me again. Just as he thought of me, he could see my head looking at him from on top of the buffet table. I was holding a finger over my lips, telling Jerry not to give away that he could see me. It gave him chills. The lad guessed he was about to have a heart attack.

"Did you shoot down a lot of planes?" Jerry asked.

"Give it a rest," Dick said. "Don doesn't want to talk about the war."

"I flew a bomber, Jerry. You knew that."

"Were you scared?"

We were scared, flying through the flak."

"Flak?"

"What is 'flak,' Don?" Dick asked.

"'Flak' was the vest we wore—a flak jacket—to protect us from shrapnel from ground cannons, the ack-ack guns."

"Ack ack?" Jerry asked.

"Antiaircraft guns, or *ack ack* to us."

Don put his fork down and raised his hands like he was holding a machine gun.

*"Flak exploding around my bomber wing."*

"It's how they sounded—*ack-ack-ack-ack-ack*. They could knock out engines, hit our fuel tanks, kill our gunners or crew."

Mesmerized, Jerry let his fork fall out of his hand and onto his plate with a clang.

"Jerry, eat," Missus said. "Let Don enjoy his meal."

*Lead bomber (second from top) being hit—March 18, 1945*

Jerry looked over at ole Charlie here's head on the buffet table almost as if I was eating with them at the table.

"Charlie," the lad said. "If Hitler and Mussolini were bad, why did God let them shoot down our planes?"

"Charlie?" Missus asked.

"Gulp!"

"Who's Charlie?" Dick asked.

"I meant *Mom*. Did I say *Charlie*?"

"You said *Charlie*," Dick said.

"Crazy me. I meant *Mom*."

The lad scrambled.

"Mom, why did God let them do those things?"

"As soon as we get back, you're seeing Dr. Brudney, young man."

"Huh?"

"You heard me."

"Cheece, a guy can't get his mail when it comes, and now I can't ask questions," Jerry groaned to himself in a whisper.

"You had nightmares last night, and now you're talking to yourself. You need a looking at by a doctor," Missus said. "As soon as we get home."

"It's puberty, Mom," Dick said. "Jerry's going nuts. I only got pimples."

After the meal, a switch went on in Jerry's brain. He didn't have much time. They were leaving for Delphi Falls the next day.

Ole Charlie was planning a busy afternoon for Don and Jerry. Jerry just didn't know what, how, or when.

# CHAPTER 14

## SECRET CODES AND ANGEL MESSAGES

"Don and Jerry, take the children into the living room and keep them busy while Aunt Mary and I clear the table and cut pies," Missus said.

Don picked up the cipher wheel in one hand and his cup of coffee in the other and went to his easy chair. He turned the cypher about and twisted the wheels. He examined the lettering and the numbers, looking for clues.

"Come help in the kitchen, Dick," Missus said.

"Why me and not Jerry?"

"Jerry's been waiting all week to talk with Don. We're leaving tomorrow. Let them be."

Dick passed a sneer to the lad.

Jerry was on the living room floor, looking at the New York State Fair's Ferris wheel on Mary's postcard and opening his letter from Mayor.

"Did you use codes when you were on your B-17 missions?"

"Code words, code names—they'd change them sometimes in case the enemy had broken them. Let me figure this cipher wheel out. Give me a minute with it."

"I can't read this postcard. It's in code," Jerry said.

"Hand it here. This thing might break the code," Don said.

Postcard in hand, Don stood from the easy chair and walked to a tall secretary desk. He sat down and took a pen in his hand. He started turning the wheels on the disk to match Mary's code letters until he saw they formed complete words on another line.

96

Mary's message was simple.

*"Send me a postcard. I collect them. Mary."*

Unbeknownst to Jerry at the time, while Don was stepping to the desk before he sat down with the postcard, ole Charlie here did some manipulating on the postcard and added more coded lines to Mary's message in her handwriting. Lines only Don would see, and they would disappear if he set the postcard down when he was finished with it. I did that knowing it was in his nature to help, so I included the message to see if he would.

While Don tried to decipher the code on the postcard, Jerry opened the letter from Mayor and read it out loud.

> *Dear Jerry,*
>
> *Conway and Marty built the cipher in woodshop. Arrange the letters to read a sentence on one of its lines. Turn the cipher thing around and write down the letters on any other line as your code. It's easy. When the other end sets a line on their cipher wheel to your code line, they'll turn the thing around, and your message will come up on another line. It'll be the only line with words, so they can't make a mistake. Be careful down there. Tell Dick to watch his mouth. I didn't say that—somebody else did—but it's a good idea. Be careful!*
>
> *Mayor.*

Jerry scratched his head.

"Did you understand any of that?"

"Come here a sec," Don said.

Jerry jumped up.

"I figured out the code. It took more than one cipher wheel line," Don said.

"Read it," Jerry said.

*Send a postcard. I collect them. Mary.*

*Go to Mission Methodist. Ask them what they need for their poor, so Aunt Lucy can send it.*


"I know Aunt Lucy," Jerry said. "Me and Holbrook put up her clothesline."

"We have to go," Don said.

"Where?" Jerry asked.

"To Mission Methodist," Don said.

"What's Mission Methodist?" Jerry asked.

Don picked up the telephone directory and looked it up. He grabbed his hat.

"Get in the car."

"Now?"

"Mary?" Don asked. "We'll be right back. Something's come up."

"Who'll watch the kids?" Aunt Mary asked.

"Get Dick to watch them."

Don waved the coded postcard in Aunt Mary's direction as if it was in semaphore, and set it on the secretary desk.

"I have a feeling this is important," Don said. "They're leaving tomorrow. Jerry and I have to do this today. I'll explain later."

Since the postcard's message was written in code, Don felt compelled to act on it. He couldn't explain why. Ole Charlie here knew why. It was Don's nature to help. It was his nature to do heroic acts.

Jerry imagined the ride like a ride in a B17, with Don piloting, resting one arm on the steering wheel and one on his knee. They drove like there was no time to spare, careful to watch for street signs, stop signs, and clues for the next turn. Their journey took them into a poorer section of Little Rock by the tracks near where Anna Kristina was born in 1937.

The Oldsmobile pulled to a stop. The Mission Methodist Church stood tall and proud, in need of paint but a beehive of activity.

Don turned the engine off.

"Come with me," he said.

They stepped from the car, walked to the bottom step of the church, pausing and looking around. People were standing about—all ages, ladies on the steps in holiday hats, choir singers in starched robes. Don tipped his hat to two women standing and talking. They stopped and waited for him to speak, as he was interrupting their Thanksgiving go-to meeting day.

"May I ask you ladies who's in charge?"

"We're a church, sir. Ain't nobody in charge."

"God's in charge," a voice said.

He had a sense there was something intimidating about a tall man in a tie from some uptown vicinity poking around their church, their safe zone.

"Ladies, a lady in a church group up north has asked that we inquire as to where northern ladies might send packages for your poor box, missions, and other offerings. It's an outreach program, I suppose. Who might I talk to about that—would you know?"

The ladies looked at each other and then back at Don, sizing him up. He had the look of a man with integrity, it seemed to them, and his shoes were polished, and his fingernails were clean.

"Sarah Wilkins might help you," a lady said.

She pointed her white-gloved hand.

"By the front door."

"Much obliged, ladies," Don said.

"Sarah's in the black dress and black hat," the other lady said.

"Thank you," Jerry said.

Don tipped his hat and made his way up the steps. Again tipping his hat and holding it over his heart, he introduced himself and Tall Jerry to Sarah and explained why they came.

Not only did the lady write her name, the church address and the sorts of items they needed, she looked up at the sky as though she had just remembered something to ask Don. It was a question she had no idea ole Charlie here was suggesting she ask.

"Sir, do you happen to know a man in North Little Rock who flew bombers in the war?" she asked.

Don was startled.

"How did you know I was a bomber pilot, ma'am?"

"Lawdy me, I didn't," she gasped.

"I was, in the war."

"Why, I don't even know what made me say that."

She looked down at her purse and then up at Don.

"Were you a bomber pilot, sure enough?"

"I was. But I don't know any pilots in North Little Rock. I know one pilot vet, Hal Hoffman, in Carlisle, east toward Memphis, but he runs a crop-dusting service."

"He isn't doing well at all," Sarah said.

"Who isn't?" Don asked.

"The man in North Little Rock—the man who flew bombers."

"What do you mean, he's not doing well?"

"It was the war. Did something to him."

"The war did something to a lot of people, ma'am."

"Not like what it did to that boy."

"Do you know his address?"

"His name is Aaron."

"Where do I find him?"

"I'll write his address down."

"Are you related to him, ma'am?"

"I knew his momma. My best friend since we was little girls sharing rain-barrel washtubs for our baths."

"I see."

"She passed in '42—passed with a heart attack, they say, but I think it was a broken heart."

Tall Jerry turned a full 360 turn, looking for ole Charlie here. He knew I was there, but he didn't know where.

"Holy Cobako," Jerry mumbled to himself.

"God bless her soul," a voice said.

"Praise Jesus," another said.

"If you go see him, mister, see if Aaron knows where his baby sister is."

"Baby sister?"

"Anna Kristina."

"Can you write her name down, too, ma'am?"

"Test the waters. The man hasn't seen her since she was five. I didn't have the heart to tell her he's alive or where he is, with his condition so delicate. I'll write her name down in case you forget."

"What seems to be his problem?" Don asked.

A lady next to Sarah Wilkins offered some information.

"He come here one Sunday back in '47—never came back, ever," she said.

"It was his brother's and momma's deaths what started it," a voice said.

"It was the war what finally did him in," another voice said.

"He came for his momma's funeral in '42," the first voice said. "In '47 he came one time and never again."

"God bless that man," Sarah said.

"A troubled soul," the lady next to Sarah said.

"He might not answer the door," Sarah said. "Just pound 'til he does. He may be troubled, but he's a gentle enough soul. He don't bite."

"Can I tell him where his sister is?"

"Don't tell him, Sarah," came a voice.

"Do you know?" Don asked. "That might cheer him up."

"If Aaron comes here, God will have his sister waiting, He surely will. You can promise him that. The girl needs the man at this time more than ever before."

"I'll share that with him if I see him," Don said.

"But he has to want to come to her."

Ole Charlie here knew Don was a good man and maybe a bomber-pilot-to-bomber-pilot talk would open the door to help that unborn baby.

Don pulled a map from his glove compartment and handed it to Jerry to give directions to North Little Rock. Soon enough they found the address and pulled in front. Folks were out and about and setting on the porches of neighboring houses. Some in rockers visiting; some sitting on stoops and some standing, smoking pipes and cigarettes, catching up on families and grandchildren.

"Put this in your pocket, Jerry. It's the list of what the mission church needs. Get it to the right people when you get back to Delphi Falls. It has the mission's address written on it."

Jerry had a sense ole Charlie had manipulated the list.

"It says, 'Aunt Lucy,'" Jerry said. "I'll get it to her."

Don knocked on the door.

He waited a full count of twenty seconds and knocked again.

The door opened.

A man Don's age was standing in the doorway, not saying a word. He seemed annoyed by the intrusion into his privacy.

Don felt the uneasiness, but just as his B-17 crew wouldn't go home after their twenty-five missions and volunteered to stay on until Hitler was stopped, he wasn't about to walk away from a man he felt a brotherhood with as a fellow bomber pilot—a man who had a burning in his gut.

"I was with the Eighth," Don said.

"Who are you?" Aaron asked.

"B-17s—heavy bombers. *Lady Helene* was our ship in '44 and '45. You?" Don said.

Aaron looked Don over. "What do you want?"

"Thirty-three missions," Don said. "The last was—"

"I was assigned to 477th Medium Bombardment Group. B-25s. The Mitchells."

"Pilot?"

"I flew the B-25. Never shipped out, though," Aaron said.

He turned his head and looked at the doorjamb.

"They never shipped us out."

"Where were you boys stationed?"

"Selfridge Field."

"Up in Chicago?"

"In Michigan."

"B-25s?"

"B-25s."

"A sweet ship, the B-25. Important ship. How'd she handle?"

Aaron started to smile but held it back.

"Wore her like a glove," Aaron said.

Don extended his hand.

"The name's Don."

Aaron looked at the outstretched hand, and then at Don.

"Aaron," he said, shaking hands.

"Can we come in?"

"You still haven't told me what you want?"

"Can we come in and talk?"

"Come on in."

Aaron held the door for Don and Jerry to walk through.

"I don't have anything to offer you," Aaron said.

"This isn't a social visit, Aaron. We came to ask you something. This is my nephew."

"Ain't no harm in asking."

Don peered around the living room at pictures of Aaron in his uniform and of a young sailor in uniform. There were vintage studio sepias that appeared to be portraits of Aaron's mother, a kindly lady wearing a pearl necklace. He looked Aaron in the eye. In it he saw a shadow of the man in uniform in the picture on the wall behind him.

"I want to start off by apologizing," Don started.

"Why? I don't know you."

"I've been waiting a long time and for the right place to say this, don't stop me now."

"You don't even know me."

"There's no excuse for the way some people were treated in the war."

Aaron caught Don's eyes, which were looking at his military picture on the mantle and added a snide comment.

"You mean us?"

"Well—"

"Ain't you heard? We're different," Aaron said sarcastically.

"No excuse at all," Don said. "There were a lot of great talents like you, willing, trained, and able to fly with the best of us to help the fight, who never got shipped overseas for action. Not to mention there were the thousands of Japanese Americans who were locked up in internment camps. I want to apologize for all that."

"It wasn't you that did it," Aaron said.

"Let me try to make sense out of it."

"Ain't but only one sense to it," Aaron said.

Don held his ground.

"America was attacked for the first time ever and bombed by the Japanese, who killed thousands of boys and gals on a sleepy, early Sunday morning. We were scared."

Aaron lowered his head.

"Pearl Harbor."

"That was it," Don said.

"Lost William in that. He was sixteen. Lied about his age."

Don bolted back, biting his lip, and looked over at the picture of the lad in the sailor's uniform. He looked back into Aaron's eyes.

"He was my brother."

"One war in the Pacific with suicide bombers diving into our ships, sinking entire fleets. Another war on the Atlantic side, Hitler taking over Europe, killing millions of civilians—it never stopped."

"Our boys could have helped," Aaron said.

"Not a doubt in my mind—never a doubt in my mind," Don said. "There'll be a day there won't be a doubt in anybody's mind. I know the Red Tail boys helped a lot."

"That's right, that's right. There you go. The Red Tails. So, why'd they send those Red Tail pups over and not us B-25 boys?" Aaron asked. "Answer me that one."

"Those were different times," Don said.

"Not all that much different today," Aaron said.

"When it was over, Aaron, I asked Jimmy Doolittle why you guys weren't shipped out. I met the man in Washington, DC somewhere. He was giving a speech at a VFW luncheon."

Aaron sat up.

"You knew Jimmy Doolittle?"

"I met him."

"He used B-25s on his raid over Tokyo."

"I got to shake his hand."

"Why, imagine that."

"Know what he told me?"

"What'd ole Jimmy say?"

"He said that this war was the first time in the history of the planet when the entire world was at war. It was a war we could have lost. He told me Germany's propaganda people had made a movie about what a hero Hitler was in America. It showed Hitler in a ticker-tape parade in New York City. He said folks in Washington, DC gave a lot of thought about sending your men and the lingering tensions in places around the country. You know what it's like, Aaron, even today. I won't pull any punches. I respect you too much for that. Doolittle told me without a blink of his eye that Roosevelt was fighting a world war he could have lost on two fronts and that he felt he didn't need to be giving General Eisenhower in Europe or General MacArthur in the Pacific a third front."

"A third front—you mean integration?"

"Yes," Don said.

105

"I never seen it that way, sure enough," Aaron said.

"There's no excuse for what they did, but there was a reason at the time they did it," Don said.

"Hundred forty of our guys were court-martialed for speaking up and complaining about the way we were being treated and seeing no action. Wasn't right, what they did to us, but I can see it the way you put it. Doesn't fit right, but it makes sense. Thanks."

"I don't like it any more than you do."

"So, why'd they go and let the Red Tails—guys like my guys fly— but not us? Makes no sense to me."

"Red Tails were in fighter planes—no crews. For you guys to pilot a bomber and lead a crew, or even to be bombardiers with the new equipment, they would have had to commission you to a grade higher than your crews. They were worried about some of the crew members not taking orders."

"I hear that, man."

"Aaron, Jimmy Doolittle would have been honored to have had you with him over Tokyo. He would have been damned lucky to have had you."

Aaron looked up into Don's eyes to see if he was true. Seeing he was, he beamed. It was his first beam since the war—and it turned almost into a silly grin as he sat there on the ottoman.

"Me dropping bombs on a factory in Tokyo. Can you just imagine it? Oh my, oh my, wouldn't that have been something, now?"

Don looked at his watch, then at Aaron's grin.

"Aaron, is your sister in trouble? That's why we came. The Mission Methodist ladies are asking about her."

"If she's in trouble, I don't know it."

"Here's my address and phone," Don said. "People want to help."

"Can I give him my address in Delphi Falls and the telephone number in case there's trouble and we can help?" Jerry asked.

Don looked Jerry in the eye as if he was thinking of his own eagerness in the war to do something that mattered. He looked beyond Jerry to the picture of the young sailor, William, who lost his life below decks on December 7, 1941. He looked over at Aaron.

"Okay with you, Aaron?"

"Fine by me," Aaron said. "We'll trade numbers."

"You'd like meeting a friend of mine, over in Carlisle," Don said. "Hal Hoffman. He flew with me—has a crop-dusting service now."

They shook hands and Don and Jerry left. Aaron stood in his doorway, watching them.

Don stopped, turned and walked back.

"Are you doing okay, Aaron? Any way I can help?"

"I'm doing fine. See that Chevy?"

"I do. Nice car."

"It's mine. It's paid for and a taxi. I'm doing just fine."

"Aaron, you might visit Mission Methodist. Ask about your sister."

"Let me think on it," Aaron said.

"Aaron, it took us until 1920 to give women a vote. We may be slow about things, but we'll make them right in the end."

Aaron smiled.

"If you ever need a taxi," Aaron said, "you got my number."

Don gave Aaron a cockpit thumbs-up and drove away.

Jerry rolled his car window up.

"If I send a code message today, when will it get to my friends?" Jerry asked.

"There's no mail today, it being a holiday. If it goes out tomorrow it might get there by next Tuesday."

"We'll be back home on Sunday."

"Write your message, Jerry. Not in code. Tonight, call your dad collect and tell him. He'll give it to whomever you'd like."

"Could I call my friend Mary and tell it to her?"

107

Don looked over and smiled. He'd been a kid once. He remembered secrets and codes.

"Sure. It'll be my treat. That long-distance call is on me, my friend."

"Thanks, Don."

"Let's go home and get some pie."

"Wait! I just remembered. You know where Capital Hotel is?"

"We'll be driving right past it."

"Can you stop there, just for a minute? I have to run in and get something."

"What would you need from the Capital Hotel?"

Jerry lied the best he could without betraying trusts.

"I promised kids hotel postcards. Will you stop?"

"We'll stop."

Jerry hated lying to Don, but he had to.

He ran into the hotel, through the lobby, and onto the elevator.

"Floor, please."

"Three."

Jerry stepped out, turned toward room 305, and knocked.

No answer.

He knocked again.

The door opened. Hemingway stood tall with his glasses on. He smiled.

"What's your news?" Hemingway asked.

Jerry handed him the cipher.

"Take this decoder so I can send you coded messages."

Hemingway grinned approval at the intrigue. He took it from Jerry and examined it.

"Jefferson made this for the State Department to use in France. Jefferson and Adams used them regularly. It's my understanding that Franklin was jealous of it and thought it a trivial toy. He had no secrets that couldn't be discussed over a glass of wine."

"You know a lot," Jerry said.

"I never held one. Clever device."

"My friends made it."

"This is an excellent reproduction."

"Somebody went to the Smithsonian and took a picture of it."

"I'm surprised it was there," Hemingway said. "Jefferson was self-indulgent and cheap. He only donated the books that created the Library of Congress because he was bankrupt, and we bailed him out."

Hemingway handed Jerry an inch-thick stack of addressed and stamped postcards.

"Okay, Papa, here's the deal. We found her brother. He lives in North Little Rock. As soon as we find more about Anna Kristina and the name of the man at the governor's office, I'll send you a coded message. I'll send you some messages anyway, to make sure the code works."

"Want a drink?" Hemingway asked.

Jerry looked at the bureau and saw the half-empty bottle of scotch on it.

"Orange juice, son. Orange juice," Ernest said with a guffaw. He pointed to a pitcher of freshly-squeezed orange juice on the desk.

"I gotta' go," Jerry said. "Somebody's waiting. I'll find out what I can."

Hemingway extended his hand.

"Papa Hemingway, can I ask you something?"

"Anything, my friend."

"Why do people treat people mean just because they think they're different?"

Hemingway stroked his beard.

"Too many don't open books. They can't imagine faraway lands and different cultures. They'll never see the brilliance of Spanish artists, warriors and bullfighters or the undying loyalty of an Asian people to their families. They'll never know the art or the poetry of music and verse that comes from Africa—from soulful cultures that brought us jazz and the blues. People who don't know other cultures are frightened by them. Racism isn't about skin, Jerry, it's about lazy intellect—about not wanting to know or care about other cultures, habits, traditions, and beliefs."

"Books?" Jerry asked. "Books are hard, sometimes."

"Reading is exercise for the brain, Tall Jerry. You have to think to read a book. Movies program a brain. They draw the pictures for you. They don't exercise the brain."

"So, if people learned about cultures like you say, there wouldn't be any problems?"

"Maybe not quite that easy. *Homo sapiens* is the only animal species that kills for pleasure. Up until now, mostly the males have killed, but that will change in time."

"Can I ask you something?"

"Anything."

"Promise you won't laugh?"

Hemingway lowered his eyelids in impatience.

"What does it mean, you know, the 'statutory' word, like what happened to the girl, Anna Kristina? What does it mean?"

Hemingway straightened, stepped back giving Jerry a gentle, curious smile.

"Your parents haven't had that talk with you, have they, Tall Jerry?

"Talk?"

"The birds-and-bees talk."

"No," Jerry said, fidgeting.

Hemingway smiled.

"Make a note to ask them to, but if I were you..."

"You're kidding, like ask my dad?"

"Wait until after New Year's. These things are best learned with a new start. New Year would be good."

"I'll think about it."

"But welcome aboard anyway," Hemingway said, smiling.

"Huh?"

"Welcome aboard life's boat, Tall Jerry, my friend. You've got what it takes to make it one hell of a ride."

He shook Tall Jerry's hand as a friend.

Jerry walked the hall, waved over his shoulder, stepped on the elevator, and went back to the car.

Don didn't say a word. He watched Jerry stuff postcards into his back pocket as he drove off.

"Why do they treat people the way they do down here, Don?"

"What do you mean?"

"Dick and I took the bus downtown and signs said who could drink from a fountain or go in to a restaurant and who couldn't—that kind of thing."

"I know," Don said.

"They wouldn't let us sit in the balcony at the movie—they said it was for other people only."

"That's a question for the ages," Don said. "I work in public health. I see it daily. I don't think people want to be cruel. I think they're trained like that from hundreds of years of family traditions. And it's not only in the south. There were slaves in New York and in places that would surprise you."

"Slavery in New York?"

"Slavery is how it started," Don said.

"I liked your story about the war," Jerry said.

"I've wanted to say what I said today for a long time," Don said. "I never ran into a fellow pilot with his story to tell before today. Quite a story…but what say we put this all behind us for now and go get some pie and look at that decipher wheel? I'll show you how easy it is. It's a great gadget. Where did it come from, anyway?"

Jerry didn't tell Don he'd given the cipher to Hemingway. He'd come up with a distraction if Don brought it up again.

"Will you guys come up for Christmas?" Jerry asked.

"Probably," Don said.

By the time Jerry had eaten two pieces of pumpkin pie and one piece of apple pie, he barely had stomach for the two scoops of ice cream Missus served up, which she never would have done had she known how much of the missing pie he was responsible for. Between the Thanksgiving meal and reliving in his mind meeting ole Charlie here and Ernest Hemingway, along with the pieces of pie and two scoops of ice cream, his body required a late-afternoon sunset nap to let things settle.

Jerry stretched out on his cot, napped through supper's turkey-sandwich snacks and didn't wake up until after dark, when it was time to go to bed. When he woke in the vacant apartment, it was quiet. There were no noises downstairs. A house with a new baby beds down early to prepare for early-morning wake-ups.

Messages to Mary would have to wait. He'd personally deliver the list from Mission Methodist when he got back. For the moment he was happy his hero Don and Aunt Mary would be coming to Delphi Falls for Christmas. He couldn't have asked for a better Christmas present. He couldn't wait to show Don off to his friends.

He sat up in the dark.

"Charlie, are you up here?"

"Charlie?"

Ole Charlie here didn't appear, but I heard the lad.

"I did good today, Charlie. Thanks for your help."

Missus, Dick, and Jerry were on the road driving north by seven in the morning's early dark.

Jerry leaned his head over, peering through the backseat window, looking for the North Star.

## CHAPTER 15

# THE DELPHI FALLS,
# A WELCOME SIGHT AND SOUND

At dusk on Sunday, Big Mike stepped out on the porch and waved a stretched arm at the gray '53 Chevy coming in the drive. Jack and Major looked up and trotted behind the car. Big Mike grinned as the car pulled around behind the swings and came to a stop. He nodded when he saw Dick driving, Missus in the front seat, and Jerry in the back. He could see the relief of being home in faces when Dick turned the engine off.

His grin was his greeting.

"How far did you drive today?" Big Mike asked.

"We stayed in a motel near Cleveland last night," Missus said. "It's good to be home."

"Did you drive all that way, Dick?"

"Today? No. Mom drove to Rochester, I drove from there," Dick said. "We took turns all the way."

Big Mike shook his hand, congratulating him. He was proud. He gave Missus a welcome hug and a peck. He rubbed Tall Jerry's head, welcoming him home.

"There's no snow," Jerry said.

"Let's not rush it," Big Mike said.

Tall Jerry stepped over to say hello to the horses.

"Take the bags and boxes inside," Big Mike said

"Leave them in the living room," Missus said, "I'll separate what needs to be washed."

"Anything to eat?" Dick asked. "I'm starving."

"Plenty of leftovers," Big Mike said.

Jerry walked back to the car, opened the door and reached onto the back window ledge.

"Mom, have you seen my cipher?"

"Look under the seat."

"It's not in the car."

"I don't have it, dear."

Jerry closed the door behind him, catching Dick's eye.

"You probably left it in Arkansas," Dick said.

Jerry opened the car door again and searched the front and the back before he remembered Hemingway. He slapped his forehead.

"I'm such a lamebrain," he muttered.

"Jerry, go see if Holbrook is still up at your camp," Big Mike said.

"Was he here?" Jerry asked.

"Invite him down for supper if he still is," Big Mike said.

"How long has he been camping out?"

"I gave him a can of Spam and some eggs yesterday. My guess is he's still there or hiking the falls. Give him a shout."

Jerry watched the cliff across the creek as he walked toward the waterfalls. He was looking for where the spring dripped water down the cliff. The camp was on top of the cliff, next to the mouth of that spring. He cupped his hands together and blew a mourning-dove call signal.

"Whooo-weee-hooo-hooo-hooo!"

He waited a few seconds.

"Whooo-weee-hooo-hooo-hooo!"

He looked up and there was Holbrook, on top of the cliff, waving. Jerry motioned for him to come down and pointed at his mouth, indicating supper. Holbrook turned, disappearing into the woods. Jerry walked back to Big Mike and Missus.

"He has to put out the campfire, but he'll be down."

"Go wash up. We'll eat when he gets here," Big Mike said.

"I'm going to put oats out for Jack and Major," Tall Jerry said. "I'll be there in a second."

He was making reacquaintances with his horse when Holbrook appeared at the front gate and strolled up the drive.

"Did you ride Jack while I was gone?" Jerry asked.

116

"I rode him last week, waiting on the spaghetti dinner. I knew you'd be home today, so my dad dropped me off."

"You had spaghetti here?"

"We all did."

"When?"

"We met here to read your letter to see what you were panicky about."

"Shut up! I wasn't panicking."

"Your dad made spaghetti."

"Oh."

"So how was it?"

"How was what?"

"The Mississippi River. Is it as big as they say?"

"Bigger. Muddy looking. It looks brown."

"Did you see riverboats?"

"We saw two steamboats in Memphis. I saw barges. Tugboats push the barges. There was a steamboat in Cincinnati, but that was on the Ohio River, not the Mississippi."

"It must have been cool," Holbrook said.

"Did my dad see the letter? It was secret."

"It was no big deal. We worried about you."

Jerry patted Jack on the neck, and then they walked to the house.

"Pull a chair. There're plenty of leftovers," Big Mike said.

"Did you roast a turkey, Dad?" Dick asked.

"Mike came from Lemoyne with his girlfriend. He cooked the whole meal."

"Gourmet Mike cooked this?" Jerry asked.

"Yes," Big Mike said.

"Wait till you meet Don, Holbrook. He flew bombers—big bombers."

Holbrook seemed preoccupied.

"I know, you told me," he muttered.

He looked at the morsel on his fork. Holbrook has been an aficionado of Big Mike's spaghetti and sausage. He'd often named Big Mike's Italian sausage as his favorite food of all time. He lifted a fork with bread stuffing on it and looked over at Big Mike.

"These gray-black things in the bread stuffing—are they your sausage, the gray-black things?"

Big Mike looked at his watch. "It's a gourmet stuffing," he said.

From that point on, there wasn't a fork lifted by Holbrook or Tall Jerry that wasn't carefully examined and smell tested. It was a slow process getting to the pie after supper.

"I bet you boys will be happy to get back to school tomorrow," Missus said.

"The Christmas dance is coming up," Dick said.

"Who're you asking?" Holbrook asked.

"I don't know. Maybe Donna Cerio, if she hasn't been asked. Did you ask anybody?"

"Judy Finch," Holbrook said. "She said yes."

"She's a beauty," Dick said.

"I think Randy is going to ask Mary Margaret," Jerry said.

"We're supposed to bring a tree ornament," Holbrook said.

"When?"

"We make it ourselves," Holbrook said. "To hang on the tree. Mary's on the decorating committee."

Big Mike and Missus were enjoying having the household together. They knew the culture shock Dick and Jerry had experienced seeing Jim Crow.

The telephone rang and Jerry went into Missus and Big Mike's bedroom to answer.

"Hello?"

"Jerry?'

"Mary?"

"I was calling your dad to see when you would be home."

"We got here two hours ago."

"Are you okay?"

"I'm okay."

"You didn't like Arkansas, huh?" Mary asked.

"It was all right. Some of it was weird," Jerry said.

"I'm sorry."

"I brought you a postcard."

"Can you get some guys to help us with decorations?"

"Sure. When?"

"Any night this week. We want it up for the dance, and that's a week away," Mary said. "My dad will drive you."

As she was talking, Jerry looked like he was starting to remember the full impact Little Rock had had on him. It was still like a dream to him. He needed a chance to think it all through.

He blurted the first thing that came to his mind.

"I got the address you wanted," he said.

"What address?" Mary asked.

"We went to that church, and a lady gave us a list of things they need for their poor box."

"What are you talking about?" Mary asked.

"I'll give it to you tomorrow."

"What church?" Mary asked.

"On your postcard. You said to go to that church and see what Aunt Lucy could send for their poor box."

As soon as Jerry mentioned Aunt Lucy, he slapped his forehead, remembering ole Charlie here must have added notes to her postcard. The lad was stuck in a hard place, trying to think how to get out of it without telling Mary about seeing me.

"I lost the cipher. Where did you buy that one you sent me?"

Jerry couldn't tell anyone he'd given his to Hemingway. They would lock him away in a loony bin.

"Conway and Marty made them."

"Can I get another one?"

"You can have mine. I just used it to send you that postcard."

119

"Thanks."

"My postcard never said what you said about Aunt Lucy."

Jerry stalled to think. He had spoken without thinking.

"Are you sure?"

"I'm sure."

"It had to, why would I make that up?"

"Do you have it? Look for yourself—it never said that."

"Hang on. I'll go look," Jerry said.

Jerry put the telephone receiver to his chest and stood, stalling.

"I have it," he said. "It doesn't say that. My mistake."

Jerry scratched his head. "I'm such a numb-nuts," he mumbled to himself. "Anyway, I got a list to give to Aunt Lucy."

"That'll be nice," Mary said. "She sends things to the needy. She'll be happy."

Jerry scratched his head.

"It's like a miracle," Mary said. "I must have told you she needed things before you went to Arkansas."

"That must be it," Jerry said.

"Maybe we can get more kids to bring things that Aunt Lucy can send those folks," Mary said. "Anyway, I'll see you in school."

"See ya."

*Click.*

Jerry avoided having a heart attack after blabbing and went to the supper table, trying to figure out when, if ever, he'd be able to bring up ole Charlie and the big mess in Little Rock.

He put the thought away when the lemon meringue pie came.

# CHAPTER 16

## THE CHRISTMAS DANCE

Jerry had mailed postcards to Hemingway by December.
The first was his code name.
"My code name is 'bullfight," the coded message said.
"HMDGWVEDYRBIRVXPH."
The second was his telephone number, New Woodstock 78.
"JSQCGAQYXVAPJR."
The third postcard, the name of the waterfalls, Delphi Falls.
"QSBFUVAXBIY."
The messages were his way of letting Hemingway know he was waiting to find something out and not to give up on him.

As the weeks went by the Little Rock episode began to fade from his memory.

Despite snow flurries, Jerry and his friends were experiencing the fun of being in high school, even if ninth graders were low on the upper classmen's totem pole. Their first high school Christmas dance. With the decorating of the gymnasium and the dance itself, the young ones were getting into the Christmas spirit.

The dance began with a freeze under a full moon as people crunched across the lawn and walked into the school. They were greeted by Ted Knapp, Mary, Mayor, and Duba standing on top of a table, singing carols. "*Hark! The Herald Angels Sing*," they chorused.

Dick bent over, slapping strings on a washtub bass. Conway and Dwyer on either side of the table were shaking sleigh bells in rhythm, slapping a tambourine on one hip.

Tall Jerry danced the fox-trot Big Mike taught him. He'd sway like a tall sunflower stalk in a late summer breeze. Graceful as she was, Donna Cerio kept up, steering him around the floor when he danced backwards. Missus had tried to teach him the waltz, but he fox-trotted to that, too.

Holbrook did the slow dances with Judy Finch. He was partial to them, avoiding jitterbugs, which weren't natural to him. They might mess his hair. During a bathroom break, Tall Jerry found Holbrook, Mayor, and Randy and belched out a twelve-year-old, "Wow, wow, wee!"

"What are you yipping about?' Holbrook asked.

"Slow dancing is the best thing ever invented."

"You got that straight," Mayor said, pulling a paper towel from the dispenser.

"I thought roller-skating was fun," Randy said. "A guy can only hold a girl's hand roller-skating."

"Man does Judy ever smell good," Holbrook said. "It must be some imported French perfume."

Holbrook took his comb, held it up, decided his hair was perfect and put it back in his pocket. He went into song.

*"I've got the world on a string, sittin' on a rainbow. Got the string around my finger…"*

"You ever think in a million years we could hold a girl for so long?" Jerry asked.

"And so close, too," Mayor said.

"And not get clobbered," Barber said.

At the punch bowl, Judy Clancy ambled over while the lads ladled refreshments.

"Hi, guys," she said.

"Hey, Judy," Jerry said.

"What's going on?" Randy asked.

"You look nice," Mayor said.

"You're sweet, thanks. I have an idea."

"Shoot," Holbrook said.

"It'd be a shame for this beautiful tree and pretty decorations to sit alone in the dark through our Christmas vacation."

"I never thought beyond the dance," Jerry said.

"You never thought beyond the girls," Mayor said.

"I was thinking the church in the hamlet could use some decorating. This tree all decorated like it is and lit up pretty would make our midnight service on Christmas Eve special. Mary and I sing with the choir."

Conway walked up with dancing the bunny hop in his smile.

"How'd we get a tree all decorated down to the hamlet without ruining it?" Barber asked.

"We'd stand it upright," Conway said.

"Huh?" Barber asked.

"They don't call me Minneapolis Moline Conway for nothin', bub. We'll put it on our hay wagon standing up, you dimwits hanging on to it, holding her steady."

"That might work," Holbrook said.

Judy pinched Conway's cheek.

"Isn't he adorable?" she asked, grinning with squinty eyes.

"He's peachy," Holbrook said.

"Let's do it tonight," Conway said. "I'll go get the tractor."

"I'm not ready to give up on a night of holding a girl and smelling imported French perfume," Holbrook said.

"Tomorrow then," Conway said.

"We can't do it until Monday," Judy said.

"Why not?" Conway asked.

"Tomorrow's Saturday, and some girls are going to Syracuse, and we have choir practice Sunday."

"Holbrook makes a good point," Conway said, looking over at freckle-faced Judy. "We'll do it Monday. School is out. We'll do it Monday morning. Now, we bunny hop."

Don and Aunt Mary would be driving in as early as Monday, and Jerry was excited. But for the moment, all he could hope for were a silver-dollar moon and a long goodnight kiss—after his first high school Christmas dance.

# CHAPTER 17

## THE MONDAY AFTER

Winter set in. Ten or more were standing about rubbing sleep from their eyes in a darkened gymnasium.

"Oh, what a night," Tall Jerry said.

"I still smell the perfume," Holbrook said.

"Whose idea was it to get such a tall tree?" Mayor asked.

"I saw it up on Driscoll's hill," Mary said.

"Sweetie pie," Judy Clancy said. "Can we move it?"

"Let me think," Conway said.

"Well *sweetie pie*, it won't get through the doors," Holbrook said.

"If we lay it down, the ornaments will fall off or break," Mary said.

"I'm thinking," Conway said.

Marty stepped to the tree and turned like a college professor.

"Wrap it in burlap. Wrap it tight to hold the decorations and ornaments."

"Will that hold them?" Judy asked.

"They may come loose, but they won't break, and we won't lose them."

"Jimmy?" Judy asked.

"Once she's wrapped, we lay her down, carry her out, set her on Conway's hay wagon and haul her to the hamlet," Marty said.

"That'll work," Conway said.

It was early afternoon by the time the Christmas-tree caravan of Mr. Vaas's truck loaded with kids and Conway's tractor was

125

underway, heading toward the hamlet of Delphi. Holbrook had to pee. Conway stopped and told him to go behind the maple on the side of the road. Holbrook announced he couldn't pee in public. Conway gave him the option of taking care of business behind the maple tree or walk.

That worked.

The Christmas tree was soon standing in front of the hamlet church. A ladder stood on either side of it, Barber balancing on one, Randy on the other, straightening ornaments and adjusting the lights. Judy Clancy was untangling an extension cord when the green 1949 Oldsmobile pulled in front of the church and let out quick honks of the horn.

"They're here!" Jerry shouted.

Aunt Mary was in the back seat with the baby.

Don left the motor running and stepped out of the car.

"Hi, Don!" Jerry said.

Don extended his hand. "Merry Christmas," he said.

Jerry made the introductions. Each in turn waved a greeting.

"That's Barber on that ladder, Randy on that. Mr. Vaas is inside checking the fuse box. This is Holbrook, Mayor, Bases, and Conway. Over there is Mary, and that there is Judy Clancy. There's more somewhere."

"Hello. We were driving by and saw you and stopped before we headed to the falls.

"I'll be home soon," Jerry said.

"Jerry, your Aunt Mary has something to tell you," Don said.

"Huh?" Jerry asked.

"She was going to wait, but this is as good a time as any."

Don opened the car door and asked Jerry to get in. He closed the door behind him, turned, and made small talk with Jerry's friends.

Tall Jerry got out of the car, beaming a smile.

"Don, were you in on it?"

126

"I confess. I know how disappointed you were when you came to Little Rock."

"What's going on?" Holbrook asked.

"Aunt Mary gave me my Christmas present."

"Where is it?" Holbrook asked.

"Her present to me is twenty-four hours with Don."

"You mean like he's your servant?" Mayor asked.

"This Don. He flew B-17s in the war. It's like we can get him to tell us about what it was like flying B-17s and bombing Hitler and that stuff," Jerry said.

"That's a neat present," Holbrook said.

"Wow?" Mayor asked. "Can we be there, too?"

"Everybody can be there," Jerry said.

"When?" Randy asked.

"Where?" Barber asked.

"She said twenty-four hours. I guess…well… Don, when can we do it?"

"It's your twenty-four hours, Jerry. Any time you say."

"Who here wants to hear Don's B-17 war stories?"

Hands went up.

"Where can we do it?" Jerry asked.

"How about in the church?" Judy Clancy asked.

"Our pond froze," Conway said. "We'll build a bonfire, hear stories and skate."

"You don't have a pond," Mary said.

"The flat at the bottom edge of the cornfield. Rain soaks it in the fall. The freeze makes it a good skating rink."

"What's the plan?" Don asked.

"How about we get our skates and meet up at Conway's in two hours?" Jerry asked.

"I'll give rides to anybody who needs them," Mr. Vaas said.

"I can take a load," Don said.

"What are the rules?" Jerry asked. "Can we ask you anything about the war, even if it's secret?"

"Ask me anything, and if it's secret and I can't tell you, I'll let you know."

"Sounds fair," Mayor said.

"There're two conditions," Don said.

"Conditions?" Jerry asked.

"First, for every question I answer about my war experiences, one of you has to tell a story of your own about the war—something you remember."

"We can do that," Randy said. "What's the second condition?"

"If I don't want to talk about something, I just won't talk about it."

Wasn't a person there who didn't understand that. There were parts of that war we remembered and parts we wanted to forget.

"Girls?" Aunt Mary shouted from the car.

Judy Clancy and Mary stopped what they were doing with the extension cord and turned.

"Try using wax paper. Tie it with string around the electrical sockets. You'll have a better chance of their not shorting out."

"Gee, thanks," Mary said.

Judy Clancy smiled and waved.

The time had been established, and the terms had been set.

# CHAPTER 18

## MARSHMALLOWS AND MESSAGES

Conway's bonfire glow could be seen over the horizon while driving up Cook's hill. Behind his milk barn on the flat of the cornfield, he and Dwyer had laid long timber logs around, so people could sit on them and lace up their skates. On a nail keg rested a paper sack filled with marshmallows. Eight long roasting sticks, their ends whittled to a point, were leaning on the keg for the taking.

There were maybe twenty-five kids milling about the fire, laughing, joking, and talking about Friday night's dance.

Don didn't like talking about the war, but he knew what a hero he was to Jerry. He looked up at the stars, watching sparks take flight. He found the log he would be sitting on, looked at Jerry and offered a friendly salute.

"At your service," he mouthed.

"Jimmy, does everyone know why we're here?" Jerry asked.

"They all know," Conway said.

"Who wants to go first?" Don asked.

Jerry stood up to get people's attention.

"Everybody, this is my uncle, Don. He flew in a B-17."

"He helped make it safe for all of us," Mr. Vaas said.

People around the bonfire smiled a welcome.

"Does everybody know the rules?" Jerry asked.

"Tell us," Barber said.

"We ask him anything, but then we have to tell a war story."

"Can I start?" Conway asked.

"Go ahead," Don said.

"Were you a pilot or a part of the crew?" Conway asked.

"I was the pilot. It was our tenth mission when the lead plane got shot down and our plane, *Lady Helene,* became the lead plane for the rest of the missions."

"Thank you," Conway said.

"Your turn," Don said.

"I remember in the early forties, maybe '43, a soldier came to school and told us how the army paratroopers needed parachutes and life preservers. He told us they were starting a drive for the floss—the pods from milkweed plants. Milkweed grows wild all around here. They paid ten cents for a big bag of milkweed floss pods. I collected a lot of sacks. My mom dropped 'em off in Apulia Station."

"Me too," Dwyer said. "I collected a lot of bags."

"Next question," Don said.

"Were you drafted or did you join, and how old were you?" Bases asked.

Don pointed the stick with a roasted marshmallow at Judy Clancy, offering her the charred, sweet delight so he could talk.

"I was a latecomer. I was eighteen in '44 when I got my draft orders. I joined the Army Air Corps. After basic training and flight school we flew from South Dakota to Long Island to rest and fuel up and then we flew the Atlantic to our base in Eye, England."

"Your turn, Bases," Jerry said.

"I remember listening to shortwave signals on our radio in the dark and thinking we would get attacked," Bases said.

"Did you fly over the Crown in your bomber?" Mayor asked.

"As a matter of fact," Don said, "we did fly over Rochester, so I could tip my wings for my mom and dad, and we were ordered to follow Route 20 over to Schenectady and then down the Hudson River to Long Island. There were a lot of us in the air, when we spread out, so some of us could have flown over the Crown."

Mayor stood.

"I remember hearing the rumbling of bombers flying over and being so scared my brother and I would hide under the corn crib. I cried until they passed over."

Bases stood.

"I remember that, too. I would get flat on the ground and not move in case they were Hitler's planes."

"I was in Cortland," Tall Jerry said. "Before we moved here. I remember standing in the backyard, crying as the sky darkened with low-flying bombers. I had nightmares."

"How many planes would fly together?" Mary asked.

"Hundreds," Don said. "I wasn't there on D-Day, but there were ten thousand planes in the air on that day alone, flying over the channel. My crew has flown with as many as two-three thousand planes."

"Why did you guys fly so low?" Holbrook asked.

"It's called 'bush hopping,' or 'flying under the radar.' We flew low so we couldn't be counted easily. Flying high could have given enemy spies time to count our planes."

"How many bombing missions did you fly?" Duba asked.

"Thirty-three."

"Did you bomb Berlin?" Holbrook asked.

"The first time we bombed Berlin our lead plane got shot down. I became lead bomber during that mission."

"Did they all die?"

"I don't like to talk about it," Don said.

"Sorry," Holbrook said.

Randy raised his hand and stood.

"I remember gasoline and sugar rationing and rubber shortages. My dad had to go to work making plane parts or something, but he wasn't allowed to tell us. The tire treads were gone. He cut an old tire into tapered strips and stuffed them inside the tires and put the tube in. That let him get to work and back without blowing a tire."

Randy looked over at his pop.

"Remember, Dad?"

Mr. Vaas nodded his head.

"Not happy times," Don said.

"They weren't," Mr. Vaas said. "Randy had to butcher chicken and skin a rabbit at four years of age. I still can't get that from my craw…having to teach him that. The women were away at Red Cross stations around the clock, working and volunteering."

"I had to stay at my grandmother's during the war," Mary said. "I remember when Daddy came home in uniform after it was over, I screamed and crawled under the bed sobbing, frightened because I didn't know who he was."

Teddy Knapp stood.

"Most farmhands had been drafted and were overseas fighting, so the army trucks would bring POWs to farms to help with the farm chores. My mother and grandmother fed them. One took a liking to me because I reminded him of his son back in Germany who was my age."

The storytelling broke into marshmallow roasting and ice-skating. Don was telling Holbrook and Jerry about the number of guns on a B-17, when a car flashed its headlights in the distance and came to a stop. Someone got out and started walking quickly down the fence line. It was Alda. She walked to Mary, leaned and cupping her hands, whispered something in her ear.

"She's there now?" Mary asked.

"Yes," Alda said.

"I thought she worked Mondays," Mary said.

"She's at our house," Alda said.

"You sure she wants me?"

"That's what she said."

Mary stood up.

"I've got to go," Mary said. "Tall Jerry, you ought to come, too."

"What's up?" Jerry asked.

"Alda, can we ride with you?"

"Sure," Alda said.

"What's going on?" Jerry asked.

"Are you coming or not?" Mary asked.

"If Tall Jerry's going, I'm going," Holbrook said.

"Us too," Barber, Mayor, Randy, and Bases all said in unison.

"I'll drive, fellas," Don said.

He waited for them to pile in. By the time he backed out, Mr. Gaines was driving Mary, Holbrook, Alda, and Tall Jerry back to his farm. He was waiting by his car for Don to pull in and park. He extended his hand.

"Welcome to our home," Mr. Gaines said.

"Nice barn," Don said.

"Call me Allen, son. Won't you come in and join the crowd?"

"Call me Don," Don said.

Except for the one bulb hanging over the table, it was a kitchen of shadows of people standing about. The waiting was suspenseful. Mrs. Gaines was standing by the sink, next to Aunt Lucy. Mary stepped to Aunt Lucy and held her hand.

"I thought you worked Mondays. Are you okay?" Mary asked.

Alda and Jackie were standing with Barber, Holbrook, Randy, Bases, and Tall Jerry.

"They gave me off today," Aunt Lucy said.

"Alda thinks you're in trouble, Aunt Lucy," Mary said.

Aunt Lucy looked down at the floor.

"These are my friends, Aunt Lucy. Whatever it is we all want to help."

Aunt Lucy put a palm over her mouth and thanked with her eyes, tipping her head sideways.

"You're sweet for being here, Mary. Everybody, thank you."

"What kind of trouble?" Mary asked.

"Not me," Aunt Lucy said. "It's a girl in another state."

Hearing Mary say 'Aunt Lucy' jogged Don's memory. He remembered her name from the visit to Mission Methodist in south Little Rock. He looked at Jerry and mouthed "Aunt Lucy?" to see if Jerry could remember hearing the name in Little Rock.

133

Jerry nodded yes.

"Listen to this letter," Aunt Lucy said.

She reached into her handbag and took several pages from an envelope. She stepped to the kitchen table, held the pages under the hanging bulb, and began reading.

*Dear Sister Lucy,*

*We can't thank you enough for the carton boxes of joy your generous friends have sent to share in our community among the less fortunate. Our souls are in God's hands, but Christmas will be a little brighter because of these gifts. The purpose of this letter to you, my friend, isn't pleasant. One of our young parishioners is in dire trouble and in need of all the prayers we can send our Lord on her behalf. Christmas will find this young lady about to give birth. I won't be mincing words, Lucy. She's a sister and sixteen, and the father is a son of an important man with the governor's office. The father sent a frightening message that they're taking this desperate girl to Forrest City Hospital near Memphis on Thursday, the twenty-fourth. He's a bad man, Sister Lucy. He's the muscle for the spineless governor who's keeping our children from getting new schoolbooks and from going to public schools. Early this week he had his own flesh-and-blood son leave two twenty-dollar bills with her to pay for the taxi to Forrest City. He told her that the state-highway patrol would know if she didn't go and that they would be following her all the way to keep her from trying any foolishness. The devil-man didn't say it, but we think that this baby won't survive this birthing. Lucy, we need your prayers. I don't have a telephone to call you, and I'm afraid to borrow one in case they listen. I don't want to bring trouble on anyone.*

*Signed,*

*Sarah Wilkins*

"The twenty-fourth," Jerry said. "That's Christmas Eve."

"Do you know the girl's name?" Don asked.

"I'm guessing it's Anna Kristina," she said. "That was the name on the list of people their church needed maternity and baby things for. Sarah wouldn't put her name in a letter like this in case."

"I understand that," Don said. "This only gives us four days."

"Are you going to help us, Don?" Jerry asked.

He nodded. "Maybe."

"Then I've got to do something right now," Tall Jerry said. "Nobody talk or ask questions. Everybody stay quiet while I do it."

"What's going on?" Don asked.

"I'll tell you after."

No one said a word.

"Mr. Gaines, may I use your telephone, please?" Jerry asked.

"Of course, son. Help yourself."

He pointed to the wall phone by the icebox.

Jerry stepped over to the phone and turned the crank twice.

"Operator, how can I help you?"

"Myrtie, this is Jerry."

"Hello, stranger. How were your travels?"

"Myrtie, I can't talk now. It's an emergency, I need help."

Whether a home had a newer pick-up-to-connect phone or an original wall-hanging crank phone, Myrtie answered. She and the party line had helped the Crown solve many mysteries in the past.

"Anything, dear. Tell me."

"I need to make an emergency telephone call, but can you charge it to my dad?"

"I don't know, Jerry. Will Big Mike go for—"

"Make the call, son," Allen said.

"Hold on, Myrtie," Jerry said.

"I'll pay for it," Allen said. "Make the call."

Jerry shook his head. It wasn't necessary.

"Myrtie. Please, it's an emergency."

There was a short pause on the line.

"What'cha need?"

"I need you to get the Capital Hotel."

"Capital Hotel?" Myrtie asked.

"That's right, the Capital Hotel. It's in Little Rock, Arkansas."

"Capital Hotel, Little Rock, Arkansas."

"When you get them on the line, ask for room number 305."

"My goodness," Myrtie said. "Are you sure?"

"Myrtie, please?"

Myrtie went quiet. Jerry could hear her patching phone plugs and connecting wires.

"Is this the Capital Hotel?" she asked.

"Yes, ma'am, how may we be of service to you?"

"Long distance for room 305, please?"

"Room 305 is not to be disturbed."

"This is an emergency call."

"I'm sorry, operator. Our guest is not to be disturbed."

"Tell them to ring room 305 and say 'Bullfight' is calling."

"Bullfight?" Myrtie asked.

"Bullfight!" Jerry confirmed.

"Did you hear that, ma'am? Bullfight," Myrtie asked.

"I just don't know," the hotel lady said.

Jerry leaned into the mouthpiece. "Lady, he's going to be mad if you don't tell him I'm on the telephone!"

Hemingway's voice came on the telephone.

"Tall Jerry, is that you?"

"Yes, sir."

Jerry said "sir" to protect Hemingway's identity. "It's hard to talk, but I found out what's going on."

"Speak slowly. Be deliberate, friend. Tell me."

"The man working with the governor's office, you know, the father of the guy who did you know what, sent her two twenty-dollar bills and told her she had to ride a taxicab on Thursday to a place called—"

Jerry looked over at Aunt Lucy for the name of the hospital.

"Forrest City Hospital," she whispered.

"Forrest City Hospital."

"That vermin," Hemingway growled.

"I still don't know his name yet, the guy or his dad's name, but he's with the governor. All I know is he told her that the state highway patrol will be following her, so she doesn't try any funny business."

"Thursday?" Hemingway asked.

"Yes."

"Christmas Eve," Hemingway said.

"I know."

"How appropriate…duplicitous cunning while the world is distracted by caroling."

"I don't know what that means, but are they going to kill her?"

Faces in the kitchen grew tense hearing the stark reality of the words, listening to Tall Jerry like they've never heard him before.

"This bastard is with the governor's office," Hemingway said. "I don't think slime like him would risk a political career with a murder that could be discovered. It's more likely they'll sedate her and the baby will be taken and given away, never to be seen in the state, ever again. They'll tell her it died during the birth."

"What can we do up here?" Jerry asked.

"Where are you, Tall Jerry?"

"Delphi Falls. My uncle is visiting. He lives in Little Rock."

"This uncle of yours from Little Rock, does he know what's going on?"

"Kind of, but no, not everything," Jerry said. "He's been telling us stories of his B-17 in the war."

"Where was he stationed?"

"In England someplace. Wait, hold on."

Jerry turned to Don. "Where were you stationed?"

"Eye, England."

"Eye, England. He flew thirty-three missions, even bombed Berlin," Jerry said.

"What rank was he?"

"He's a captain…he's a pilot."

"Tall Jerry, this could be a good piece of information."

"What do you mean?"

"Listen to me carefully."

"Okay."

"I'll wait here for instructions. I want you to turn the entire matter over to the captain. Tell him everything you know. Don't leave a detail out and let him come up with a plan. Tell him I'm here to serve in any capacity. Do we have an understanding?"

"Yes, sir."

"Are you certain you understand, Tall Jerry?"

"I'm sure."

"Call me when you need me to do something."

"Okay."

"Tell the captain everything."

"Can I tell him your name?"

There was a pause.

"Let's not, son. There may be a time, but this isn't it. We need a hero right now, not a circus."

Hemingway hung up without saying goodbye, as did Jerry.

Jerry turned toward Don.

"Here's the deal. We want to help the girl in Little Rock and her baby, and you're a captain, that's all there is to it. Will you help us?"

"Jerry, we need to talk."

"Will you help us?" Jerry asked.

"I don't know if—"

Mary stepped up face-to-face with Don.

"We may be kids to some people, but we've caught burglars who've robbed businesses. This year we caught two POWs who escaped. We caught a pickpocket. We even ran a farm for Farmer Parker because he hurt his back. We learned to do all this from the examples set by heroes like you who sacrificed your lives for our freedom."

"That's admirable," Don said. "I'm proud of you...but I have responsibilities, a job, and children."

Mary leaned into Don's face.

"Don, in all of the times we've tried to do good, in all of the times we caught or trapped bad people, never once was a person's life in danger. Not once."

"I see." Don said.

"It could be two lives in danger. We need help. Help Aunt Lucy—and that girl in Little Rock. We're begging you."

Don stared into Mary's eyes as she made her plea. He broke his stare, looked over at Jerry and then into eyes around the kitchen. He understood the discomfort Jerry felt in Little Rock, seeing the ambivalence to Jim Crow at its worst.

"I need to talk with Jerry alone," Don said.

He took Jerry by the arm, led him out the side door into the cold, and closed the door behind them.

"You lied to me!"

"What!?"

"I want to know why you lied," he snapped.

Jerry was crushed. Don was his hero and his thinking Jerry would betray him wrenched the lad's gut.

"Don..."

"You lied to me."

"I promise I didn't, Don. I would never lie to you."

"So, you had to stop at that hotel to pick up postcards, right?"

His eyes locked on Jerry's with a "gotcha."

"Oh, that," Jerry said.

"No games, Jerry. Who did you call in Little Rock?"

"I can't say. I mean, I promised."

"I can't help you then. Sorry." Don turned to go back in.

"Wait."

"There can't be secrets with something this important."

Jerry didn't want to lose his hero's confidence in him, and he didn't want to break his confidence with Hemingway, and he surely couldn't tell about ole Charlie here, so I gave him a nudge. Looking through the side-door window, Tall Jerry could see a bible resting on a table.

"Don, do you believe in God?" Jerry knew he did, but he had to make a point.

Don started and then straightened his back.

"That's a stupid…well of course."

"Do you believe in guardian angels?"

"What!?"

"Do you believe in guardian angels?"

Don relaxed his posture. He pursed his lips and nodded.

"The Nazis had special training on how to attack the B-17 with all our guns. There was flak exploding all around us. We were in real danger of bumping into one another—that many planes in the air. Missions were out for a few hours of hell and a few hours of hell back to the base. You bet I believe in guardian angels. Wasn't one mission over the channel I didn't speak with my guardian angels all the way out and all the way home. They kept me alert and awake and my crew alive. Of course I believe in guardian angels."

"Well, you're going to have to trust me now," Jerry said.

"I trust you, Tall Jerry."

"I have somebody in Little Rock who will do anything you tell him to do, but I can't tell you his name. At least right now I can't."

Don backed up the step and into the kitchen, tweaked his chin, and circled the table twice. He paused. He looked down at the seated Allen.

"What do you think, Allen?" Don asked.

"The child's in all kinds of worry. She surely is, my friend."

"Pretty helpless, it looks," Don said.

"Birthing with a man around is hard enough, but alone at her age?" Allen asked. "Lordy, the fear that must be in that chile's heart."

"Shall we?" Don asked, raising his brows in anticipation.

"I'm too old to say no. It's the least we can do…" Allen said. "'Sides, we haven't had this much excitement in this kitchen—well, for years."

Don spun about and barked. "Clear the room!"

"Huh?" Mary asked.

"Everybody leave!" Don said.

"Can't we be here?" Jerry asked. "It's not fair."

"You put me in charge. I'm setting the rules. You all must leave. Walk your friends over to the house for hot chocolate—maybe some spaghetti. Allen, the ladies and I have thinking to do. We're going to come up with a plan—a strategy."

"For real?" Jerry asked.

"For real," Don said. "We'll let you in on it when we know."

"Alda, Jackie," Mae said. "Bundle up and go with them. We'll come fetch you."

Alda looked at Mary and then at Jerry.

"Walk straight home," Don said. "You should be there in ten, maybe fifteen minutes. Don't lollygag in case we call and need you."

"After you get a plan, we can help?" Jerry asked.

"Yes," Don said.

"Are you mad at me?" Jerry whispered to Don.

"I could never be upset with someone for keeping his word," Don said.

Jerry grinned.

"Jerry, do you remember Aaron?"

"Sure, I do."

"I got him a job with my crop-duster friend, Hal Hoffman, in Carlisle."

"Fixing planes?"

"He's flying a crop duster. He dusts the rice fields."

"I thought he had a taxi."

"He does both. Now he has a smile on his face."

"Does he know about the trouble his sister is in?"

"He's about to. Take off with your friends. Let Allen and me plan. Tell your Aunt Mary I'll be late."

"I have twenty-four hours. Does this count?" Jerry asked.

Don smiled and held the door for them.

The group pulled their coats on, stepped from the house, and started walking the half mile to the Delphi Falls.

"Mae, Aunt Lucy, how about some food on the table?" Allen asked. "Our guest can't think on an empty stomach. Let's eat and socialize. Then we'll come up with something over a pot of chicory coffee and cinnamon to get this chile out of her mess."

# CHAPTER 19

## TALL JERRY SAYS GOOD BYE

Walking the hill from the Gaines's down to Maxwell's corner, Holbrook asked Jerry the big question.

"Who'd you call, Tall Jerry?" Holbrook asked.

"Later," Jerry said.

"C'mon, who were you talking to?"

"A man I met in Little Rock. No big deal. He's a good guy, is all."

"Why call him?"

"He said he'd help us."

"How'd you get in the middle of this mess?" Mayor asked.

Jerry remembered Jackie and Alda were walking with them and didn't want to make them uncomfortable. He dodged the question of what he'd seen in Arkansas.

"Long story," he said. "Not now. I already told you in my letter. I wasn't kidding."

Barber looked at Alda and Jackie. "You're lucky you're not living in Little Rock," he said.

"Why?" Jackie asked. "Is it awful down there?"

Her innocence reminding them they were ashamed of the way it was in Little Rock. They chose not to elaborate for seventh graders. Mary took the lead.

"Oh, it's nothing. Some people can be real jerks," Mary said.

They stepped through the gate of the long gravel drive to Tall Jerry's house. As they walked the drive Jerry imagined seeing lights sparkle on the barn-garage roof in the distance.

"Did anybody see that?" he asked.

143

"See what?" Holbrook asked.

"That light," Jerry said.

"What light?" Holbrook asked. "I see lights inside the house. All I can hear is the racket from the waterfalls. Is that what you mean, lights in the house?"

It was the first time in weeks that it all came back to Jerry. The boy knew if he saw a light again on the barn-garage roof, it might be a signal. He did.

"You guys go on inside, get some hot chocolate or whatever," Jerry said. "I want to check on Jack and Major, see if they have hay."

"I'll help you," Holbrook said.

"You go, too. Get some Italian sausage. I'll be in."

There was no argument from Holbrook. Jerry stood and watched them walk up to the door, knock and get welcomed in.

After the door closed behind them, Jerry walked to the side of the barn-garage where the horse-stable shed was.

He used the loudest whisper-voice he could manage.

"Charlie?"

No answer.

"Was that you flashing the light?"

No answer."

"Are you up there, Charlie?" Jerry whispered.

Ole Charlie here appeared just above the transom on the roof. Sure enough, I was standing up on top of the barn-garage in my bib overalls.

"Jerry, bless you, young man."

"Where did you disappear to, Charlie?"

"Calm down, son."

"I've been asking for you everywhere I go and looking like a fool."

"I need to talk with you, son."

"Yeah, but when I have to talk to you, nothin!"

"Come up here. It won't take long, what I have to say."

144

Jerry peered over to the house to see if anyone was looking out a window. He looked up at ole Charlie.

Jerry closed his eyes.

"Okay, I'm ready," he said.

"That's good, Tall Jerry, we'll be waiting."

Jerry opened his eyes.

"Charlie, can't you, like, do something, like, say something so I just float up there?"

"What?"

"Can't you, like, snap your finger, and I'll just appear on the roof with you?"

"I'm an angel, son. I'm not a magician."

"Oh."

"Get a ladder and take it around back so no one sees."

"I thought you said only I could see you, Charlie. That's what you said."

"No one can see me, son, but they can see you."

"Oh."

"Take a ladder around back."

"Okay," Jerry said.

"And hurry. Time's a-wasting."

The ten-foot-tall ladder swirled around about falling backward into the creek taking Tall Jerry with it. He managed to steer it back and settle it on the edge of the barn. He climbed and sat on the shingles, waiting for ole Charlie.

I must have had a prayerful look in my eyes.

"Tall Jerry, good people are about to venture into a journey of great peril and deep personal sacrifice. They're about to try to help someone—to save God's children from harm's way."

"I telephoned Hemingway, long distance," Jerry said. "I did and he promised to help, just like you said he would."

"Tall Jerry, this is important, what I have to say."

"Okay?"

145

"You have to see to it that your father knows about this."

"What!?"

"Take him aside and tell him everything."

"Like how?"

"Do it tonight."

"Tonight, do I have—?"

"As soon as you climb down the ladder and go up to the house. If he's the man ole Charlie here says he is, son, your pap will know what to do."

"He's the man, son."

"But Charlie," Tall Jerry said.

"He is, Big Mike is a special man."

"Anything else?" Jerry asked.

"You're a good lad, son. It's been a pleasure meeting you again. Heaven thanks you for your bedtime prayers. Keep them coming up. It's only fair I tell you that you won't be seeing me again after you climb down and step off the ladder."

"What do you mean?"

"Your memory will be erased, son."

"Like I won't know Charlie anymore?

"You'll remember me, you won't remember talking to me."

"Never?"

"You won't have the memory," ole Charlie here added.

"That's not fair."

"One day you'll understand, Jerry."

"Will I remember Ernest Hemingway?"

"You will, and he will help because of your courage, Tall Jerry, not because of anything we've done. The man admires you."

"It's not fair."

"You'll know this is best, son, one day," ole Charlie here said.

"So, I'll remember it someday?"

"One day perhaps, when you're closer to God you'll be better able to understand it all."

146

"Closer? I say my bedtime prayers at night, Charlie. That's pretty close."

"Perhaps 'nearer' might be the better word, son. In the meantime, you have much growing and living to do. Your life needs no more distractions from us. Your friends need the Tall Jerry they're growing up with without complications."

"It's tough, keeping it secret," Jerry admitted.

He hung onto the ladder rung, trying to get a last look at ole Charlie as an angel so he would never forget.

"Go tell your dad, son," I said. "Tell him straight away. He can help."

Jerry put his foot down on the first rung on the ladder.

"I promise," he said.

Holding the sides, he began stepping down.

"Jerry?" ole Charlie here asked.

"Yes?"

"Merry Christmas, my friend."

Jerry waved at ole Charlie here as he stepped to the ground.

"Merry Christmas, Charlie. Thank you for being my guardian angel. Bye."

The second Jerry stepped off the bottom rung and from that moment on all he could remember was running to the house in front of the Delphi Falls to tell his dad about the girl in Little Rock and about Don and Mr. Gaines meeting to come up with a plan.

# CHAPTER 20

## CORNED BEEF HASH AND EGGS OVER EASY

"Do you go by 'Don' or 'Uncle Don,' young man?" Allen asked. "And do you like cotton-fried puffballs?"

"Don's fine," Don said. "And yes, I like puffballs. How do you season them?"

Mae carried her iron skillet over and rested two puffball slices on Don's plate. He leaned in and sniffed the air about the plate.

"Ah. Bacon drippings and garlic. Maybe a touch of fennel?" Don asked.

Mae sported a curious look, wondering if Don was being truthful or just polite about liking puffballs. But it looked as though he'd guessed right on all counts, including the fennel.

"It was the year I earned my Eagle Scout badge," Don said. "When we found puffballs on a trail, one guy in the troop told us how his mom prepared them. He showed me how to clean them using my jackknife. They're great with eggs."

"I could have used you on the Pullman," Allen smiled. "You have a flair."

"Is that what you did before farming, Allen?"

"I was a Pullman man. The Chicago and New Orleans run for twenty-two years. Pullman is more than just a railroad, Don."

"Oh, you bet it is. I've seen a few Pullman cars," Don said. "They sure do know how to go first class."

"I started as a porter, but I wanted to be a chef and cook."

"Did they promote you?" Don asked.

148

"Pullman was slow on pay for some folks. Gave us about seventy-eight dollars a month. As a porter, a brother would get tips, too, but I wanted to cook. Cooked a meal for my boss man. He liked my cooking and made me a chef."

Don looked over at Allen as he told the story. He could see the smile in the old man's eyes bubbling up from his memories of many happy years on the rails.

"I bet you've seen a lot of things and met a lot of folks over those twenty years," Don said.

"Twenty-two years, son. Oh, I did see some things," Allen said. "I 'spect I saw it all, pretty much. One passenger I know'd more than eleven years gave me this here farm on a payout. He surely did."

"God bless that man," Mae said.

"Cooking his eggs, the way he liked them with a dash of chorizo I'd be telling him my dream of someday being a farmer and raising chickens and hogs and corn. Don't you know that man waited for me to step off the train in Chicago one time and told me he owned a place up in this neck of the woods and did me right by offering to carry the paper way he has? I pay him each December and will until it's paid for or die first. I never miss."

"With your travels down to New Orleans all those years, no doubt you've seen what it's been like in the South—for some folks, I mean…" Don started.

Allen chose not to address open sores. He broke a gaze and turned his head to Don.

"Do you favor corned-beef hash, son?" he asked. "I make a good corned-beef hash."

"How do you serve it, you being a seasoned chef?" Don asked. "Do you rest a poached egg on top?"

"I do. How about you?" Allen asked. "We can do two eggs if you like. We have plenty of eggs."

"I met a chef at a hotel on Long Island. Chef Josh, as I recall," Don said. "He told me the best way to eat good corned-beef hash is with an egg over easy draped on top like a saddle blanket."

"I like that idea," Allen said.

"He said it'd spread more egg goodness into the hash than one poached would. It works."

"Woman," Allen said. "How about some corned-beef hash for our friend and ole Allen here? You ladies join us if you're of a mind."

"Coming up," Mae smiled. "I'm thinking it'll be with eggs over easy?"

Don smiled.

"Aunt Lucy," Don said. "You do good work sending out those packages. I know the ladies in that church in southern Little Rock are appreciative."

"I do what I can," Aunt Lucy said. "My boss lady pays my postage for big boxes, bless her heart. I've never sent packages out of state before. Just don't know what got in me to do it this time, but the Lord has spoken, and He's given us a young girl to help."

"Praise the Lord," Mae said.

"She let me off today to come here. I pray we can help that little girl. I surely do."

"Allen," Don said. "Don't take me wrong, but I have to ask you to teach me all you can about your experiences, especially what you know about the South, having traveled through it so much all those years. I'm searching for hints or clues as to what we might be able to do to help this girl. Something maybe I can't see yet and might grab onto."

"You mean you want me to tell you what it's like to be a man like me?"

"Allen, I could write ten books about what it's like to be you in the South and I wouldn't come close to it."

"Only ten?"

"If we're going to help this girl, I sort of have to know your experience the way it is to see my options."

"I never spoke of this in this house, and I trust you'll take it on out of here when you go," Allen said.

"What we share goes nowhere," Don said.

Don extended his hand for a shake.

"You have my word."

They shook.

"In '27 a brother was hung, shot, and his body was dragged through the streets of Little Rock. The man was custodian at a church who found a dead girl in the church and ran to report it to the police. The police arrested him for the murder on the spot. They dropped his body at Ninth and Broadway. Thousands showed up, broke into his neighborhood's stores and homes, threw fixtures and furniture on the fire for kindling and burned him."

"Nineteen twenty-seven was some time ago," Don said. "It's not as intense now."

"For some folks in the South, a soul doesn't have all that many options," Allen said.

"I'm serious," Don said.

Allen reflected on it for a moment.

"One thing was certain," Allen said. "Brothers and railroads have gone together like bride and groom for a hundred years. We built them as slaves, and they hire us cheaper to ride as porters. Ya' see, folks in the South don't mind us riding through their towns on a rail or carrying their luggage. They just don't want us living too close."

"Sounds like you're saying it's an out-of-sight, out-of-mind kind of thing?"

Mae cracked an egg in the skillet and stepped over to the table as it spattered. She pointed the spatula.

"What are you thinking, young man?" she asked.

"I'm just thinking."

151

She stepped back over to her skillet.

Food was served, and silence filled the room with thoughts. As he cleaned his plate, sopping what was left with a folded piece of buttered toast, Don looked up.

"Maybe there's a way we could hide her until after the baby was born," Don said.

"I know one thing, son," Allen said. "If Jim Crow don't want that baby around, that baby won't be around long."

Don looked over at Allen as if he could feel the angst in the man's voice.

"This won't be easy," Allen said.

"Maybe we have to come up with some way to get the girl out of Arkansas altogether," Don said.

"It's been some time, but if I remember right," Allen said, "looking out the Pullman window across the Mississippi from Memphis, the highway to Little Rock is straight as an arrow. They could have highway patrol cars lined up like fence posts, watching any move she makes. It's hard enough to hide a pregnant girl from south Little Rock in the daylight, especially if they're following her. I don't see how you'll get her past all that."

"You have a point," Don said. "If the man in the governor's office is connected to hate groups, it could make it dangerous."

"We know he's connected, or we wouldn't be here," Allen said.

"Save that child," Aunt Lucy said.

"And her baby," Mae said.

"Allen, teach me what it's like to be you, in Arkansas," Don said.

"What on earth!" Mae said.

"Simmer, woman," Allen said. "I know the man's meaning."

"Think south," Don added. "Teach me you in the South."

Don leaned.

Allen rested his forearms on the table and clasped his hands. He gazed down to the tabletop, gathering his thoughts as though he was transporting himself into his memory of the South.

"Ain't no jobs lest it's little pay or no pay and a meal. Brothers there learn how to get by on their own. Some takes the good road and work several jobs to support their families, some start businesses in their vicinity."

"What's a 'vicinity'?" Don asked.

"Some folks calls it a neighborhood. Some southern folks live in the vicinity—could be the vicinity of the church, vicinity of the warehouse, maybe the vicinity of a Sears."

"Interesting," Don said.

"Some cut hair or have a ladies' salon. Some have pushcarts selling home-grown vegetables or delivering eggs or skinned rabbits. I'm up in Syracuse Saturdays selling eggs and chickens at the university and to the restaurants. By having their own businesses in cities, they're dealin' with their own and nobody outside is minding their business like some do, especially in the South."

"So, in their 'vicinities,' they have networks, ways of doing things—ways of bartering and getting things done?" Don asked.

"Yes, but for their own kind," Allen said. "A man like you wouldn't get into their circle."

"I wonder why that is," Don said.

"You just wouldn't."

"Not even if I could help them?"

"It's more than that, son."

"Tell me."

"It's about pride. If a man in that vicinity is twenty-cent an hour and a man like you is a dollar-fifty for the same hour, better you not come around. It's a reminder we ain't equal—a hurt."

"I understand now."

"At least man-to-man in the vicinity, we know we're equal, and we can understand one another."

"What could we do to help a man in a vicinity like you're talking about feel successful? What would it take?"

Allen thought and pointed to a side table.

153

"See that table yonder?"

"I do."

"The one with the books stacked on it?"

"I see it."

"That's how a man like me knows he's rich."

"Books," Don said.

"Books in the house—books that get read—mean success. Books make us rich. They're our ticket up."

"That's good," Don said.

"It's more than that," Mae said.

"Woman, what could be more than books?" Allen asked.

"A father at home and the books, too," Mae said. "Now that's something."

Allen smiled. "Woman, in all my life, it has never dawned on me to not be here for my family."

"Thank you, Jesus," Mae said.

"I can see vicinity businesses and services serving their own, Allen, but Pullman workers got outside of vicinities—outside of towns and mixed with folks. Who else in a vicinity would do that? What businesses would rely on all folks from time to time?"

"Taxicabs," Allen said.

"Taxis?" Don asked.

"You sometimes have two men chip in to pay for buying a car and share driving and go about chauffeuring near every neighborhood when they're called."

Don reflected, took his wallet from his back pocket and pulled a slip of paper from it.

"Allen, you've given me an idea. Might I use your telephone?"

"On the wall," Allen said, pointing.

"A long-distance call."

"On the wall," Allen said.

"I'll keep track of charges," Don said.

"You'll do no such thing!" Allen said. "Make your calls."

Don walked to the wall.

"Ladies, it's time for coffee," Allen said. "You might consider the large church urn, Mae—plenty of chicory and cinnamon. It could be a long night."

Don picked up the earpiece, leaned into the mouthpiece, and cranked the handle around twice.

"Operator."

"Operator, I'm making a long-distance call. I need to connect to North Little Rock, Arkansas. The number is Pulaski 407, please."

"Pulaski four, zero, seven in North Little Rock, Arkansas?" Myrtie asked.

"That's right," Don said.

"I'll connect you if they answer," Myrtie said.

"Little Rock, how may I help you?"

"Long distance calling Pulaski four-zero-seven. Can you ring it, please?"

"Are you paid, operator?"

"We're paid," Myrtie said.

"One moment, please," the Little Rock operator said. "I'll connect you."

Allen stood and stepped over to Don. He held his palm over his mouth and whispered.

"You might be careful. Somebody could be listening in."

Don winked at him, understanding his point.

"Hello?"

"There's your party," Myrtie said.

"Aaron?"

"Who's calling?"

"Aaron, it's Don."

"Hey, my man. How are you?"

"We're visiting relatives for Christmas."

"Oh, that's nice. Whereabouts are ya'all?"

Don didn't want to be overheard by someone in Arkansas.

"A small farm. We'll catch up when I get back."

"You have a good Christmas, my friend. I'll tell Hal Hoffman you called."

"How's the crop-dusting coming, Aaron?"

"It's slowed for the winter, but I'm getting good at it. It's a light plane but loaded with power. I get it to the end of the field and pull her straight up and twist and roll her down again."

"That takes power, not like your old B-25, I'm guessing."

"Oh, Don, funny you should mention, you'll never believe it."

"What?"

"Hal Hoffman was trying to get a B-17 from the army salvage, but most had been wrecked, and it was slim pickings."

"I haven't seen the numbers, Aaron, but I'd think most of the B-17s either crashed or were shot down. Heavy losses in flight-school training."

"He did find a B-25. Funny you should mention it."

"You're joking, right?"

"A B-25!"

"A Jimmy Doolittle B-25? A 'bombs-over-Tokyo' B-25?"

"Sure enough."

"I'll be."

"Sure as I'm sitting here, he found them at a war surplus in Savannah. Took me with him to look them over. I told him which one was in the best shape. I told him what parts he may be needing down the road."

"You would know."

"I got it running like a champ. He let me fly it from Savannah to the dirt strip behind the diner, the field we have for the dusters."

"What do you think of that, a B-25. How'd she feel, Aaron?"

"Took some getting used to the feel of the big old lady again, getting it back here and all, but Hal Hoffman was patient and let me take my time."

"Congratulations, Aaron."

"This winter, when I'm not driving my cab, I'm mechanic on the planes. He has two dusters and now the B-25. We built a tin hangar. I take good care of them."

"Aaron, I need to ask you a question."

"Ask, my friend."

"Don't take it wrong, but I need to ask if you've been in contact with your sister."

"No, man. Ah...well...no, man. I wouldn't know what to say."

"Aaron, I need to tell you that she may be in trouble, and she could use some help. Can't talk about it now, don't even dare say her name on the phone, but can I count on you?"

"You can count on me. Anything—just tell me. Can I ask for something, my brother?"

"Anything."

"Can you not tell her my name or anything like that, and let me do it if the time is ever right?"

"You have my word, good buddy."

"Thank you, my brother."

"Aaron, I'll call this number or Hal Hoffman's hangar if I come up with something."

"I'll be at one or the other—unless I'm out in my cab."

The two said their goodbyes and hung up.

Don turned the phone crank two more times.

"Operator."

"Operator, can you ring New Woodstock 78?"

"Big Mike's place. I sure will."

"Thank you."

"Do I know you?" Myrtie asked.

"I don't think so. I'm Tall Jerry's uncle, Don."

"Congratulations on having your baby. It's nice to make your acquaintance. I'm Myrtie."

"Hello, Myrtie."

"Connecting you."

"Hello?"

"Hello, who's this?"

"Dick."

"Dick, this is Don. Is Jerry there? I need to talk with him."

"Dad took him over to meet you. Are you at the Gaines's?" Dick asked.

"I am."

"They left half an hour ago. They should have been there by now."

"I think I hear them. Thanks, Dick. Bye."

Just as Dick said goodbye, there was a knock on the side door. Allen opened it. In stepped Big Mike, Mike Shea, Doc Webb, and Tall Jerry.

# CHAPTER 21

## DOT ON THE WALL AND VOLUNTEERS

"We're not here to kibitz," Big Mike said. "Jerry filled me in on what's going on, and we're here to help."

"Mighty thoughtful, gentlemen, but I don't have what I'd call a plan yet. Trying to put the pieces of the puzzle together with what little I know."

"Everybody," Big Mike said. "Don? Allen? Ladies? Say hello to my friends here, Doctor Webb and Mike Shea."

"We know the doctor and Mr. Shea," Allen said. "Welcome to our home, gentlemen. Help yourself to more coffee. It's a fresh pot, and there's plenty."

They made their pleasantries, took their coats off and joined Allen and sat around the table, watching Don pace back and forth in the shadows of the kitchen.

"Mae," Big Mike said. "Do you have a sheet of paper and a crayon?"

"Certainly."

She stepped from a side table and handed paper and a crayon to him. He stood up.

"Don," he said. "While you're putting things in order in your head. Mind if I help you get it kick-started?"

"I'm stuck on this one," Don said.

"Maybe we can help," Big Mike said.

"I need all the help I can get."

Big Mike took the crayon and smudged a small dot in the center of the large sheet of paper. He held it up for people to see.

159

"Don," he said. "What do you see on this sheet of paper?"

"It's a dot," Don said.

"A dot," Tall Jerry said.

"Yep, looks like a dot to me," Allen said.

"It must be a trick question," the doc said. "What's on the sheet of paper, Big Mike?"

"You see the dot. Well it's there, all right. But see all the white space around the dot. It's a full sheet of blank paper with a small dot in the middle."

"I get it," Don said. "I've been thinking the dot, or inside the box, and you want me to think outside the box?"

"Exactly, son."

"Want to give me a hint as to how I can think out of the box on this?" Don asked.

"If you dream it, you can achieve it."

"I'm not getting your point."

"What have you done so far?"

"I called the girl's brother to tell him I need his help."

"Anything else?"

"Allen has been helping me learn a culture in the south to give me some windows for possible approaches."

"Anything else?'

"Not that I can think of. No, wait—Tall Jerry called someone he knows in Little Rock who said he would help."

"It's time to dream it up," Big Mike said.

"I'm still not getting it," Don said. "I can't just dream up a plan."

"Don, elbow grease comes in cans, not cants. Pretend you're a magician and you could make anything happen with the snap of your finger. What would you do right now?"

"Anything?"

"You're a magician. Absolutely anything. Just dream it up and snap your finger."

"Well first thing is I would go down there, but it's a four-day drive, and we don't have four days."

"I forgot to tell you the magician rules," Big Mike said.

"What!?" Don barked. "Magician rules?"

"Magician rule number one, son. You can't say 'but' as a magician. No 'buts' allowed puts you in Little Rock. What next?"

"That's right," the doc said. "You're in Little Rock."

"I'd figure a way to get the girl and take her to safety."

"What next?" Big Mike asked.

"I'd hide her out until after the baby was born."

Don circled the table two times, prancing faster each time, first around the front and then around the back, past the sitting gentlemen. Ideas were stirring in him.

"Don," Mike Shea said. "How many troops would you need with you to help her to safety?"

"What do you mean?"

"How big of a team do you suppose, if you were there?"

"A woman to look after the girl. She's well along. Maybe two more to be lookouts, maybe, and to carry things, to be backups. Three in all would do it. The two already in Little Rock…that'd make five."

Big Mike looked across the table at Mike Shea.

"You thinking what I'm thinking, Mike?"

"I am," Mike Shea said. "You game?"

"I'm game," Big Mike said.

"You game, Doc?" Mike Shea asked.

"I'm in," the doc said. "Not sure what you're talking about, but count me in."

"Put your team together," Big Mike said.

"That's all well and good, but it won't work," Don said.

"And why not?" the doc asked.

"It'll take several days to get there. I'm the only one with a driver's license," Don barked.

"It'll only take a few hours to fly," Mike Shea said.

"Fly?" Don asked.

"We're putting up the money for airline tickets to fly you and your team into Little Rock and whatever expenses you have down there. Money you need for you and your team."

"You mean it?"

"Pick your team."

"Flying into Memphis would be safer," Don said.

"Man's right," Allen said.

"We'll get a rental car and drive to Little Rock."

"Man's smart," Allen said. "Highway patrol for Arkansas won't be in Memphis on the lookout, whereas they might be at the Little Rock airport."

"I like it," the doc said.

"The man knows, gentlemen," Allen said. "They won't be looking for folks coming into Arkansas, just for folks leaving."

"But either way, they'll be at the Little Rock airport looking for something. Memphis is safer," Mike Shea said.

"Pick your team, son," Big Mike said.

Don looked over at Jerry.

"Jerry?"

Jerry stood, "From now on I'm Tall Jerry, Don, and Holbrook, Mary and I are your team!"

"Not yet, Jerry."

"Tall Jerry."

"Tall Jerry, call your contact and ask him something for me?"

"Sure, I'll call him. But Holbrook, Mary and I are going with you. We're your team for Little Rock. What do you want me to say when I call him?"

"I'll write it down. Go get him on the phone."

"Mr. Gaines?" Tall Jerry asked, pointing over to the telephone on the wall.

"Be our guest," Allen said.

Jerry turned the crank around twice.

"Operator?"

"Myrtie, this is Jerry. Will you get me the Capital Hotel again in Little Rock, Arkansas, long distance, and ask for room 305?"

"I have my notes. Do I still say 'bullfight' this time?"

"If you have to, yes."

Don handed Jerry a sheet of paper with instructions.

"Tall Jerry?" Hemingway asked.

"We sort of have a plan. Want to hear it?"

"Shoot!"

"Hold on, I have to read it."

"Take your time."

Jerry read the note.

*"We'll need somebody with a car that can't be traced back to Little Rock and a driver pretending to be a cabby. He must be Caucasian, the driver, that is, and he'll pick the girl up at the Mission Methodist Church like he's the taxi she called. Then we'll need him to take her to a place that we haven't picked yet, but we'll figure it out tonight or tomorrow and tell you."*

"Done!" Hemingway bellowed. "I fit the bill. I already have the car. It's parked in the side lot of the hotel. It's a Hertz renter from the Memphis airport. They'll never trace it back to Little Rock."

"Can't they trace it to you?" Jerry asked.

"How, Tall Jerry? In case you forgot, I'm Manolin Santiago, my friend."

"That's right! I remember now. Perfect. Is that name with the car too?" Jerry asked.

"With the car, too. I'll wear my best disguise."

"You're great," Jerry said.

"No, you are, my good friend. Call with further instructions when you have them. Call me at any hour."

"I'll call, but plan for it to be this Wednesday at five o'clock. That's when you'll pick her up at the mission like you're her taxi driver taking her to the hospital in Forrest City."

"Is that where I'm to take her?"

"No, but we don't know where you'll actually take her yet. It's important that everyone where she is thinks that the hospital in Forrest City is where you're taking her."

They both hung up.

Don took the earphone from Jerry and gave it two full cranks.

"Operator."

"Myrtie, can you get Pulaski 407 in North Little Rock, Arkansas, for me, please?"

While Myrtie went through her machinations, Don turned to the group.

"I think the pieces are starting to fit together," he said.

Big Mike, Mike Shea, the doc, Allen, and the rest looked on in awe, almost as if they were in the middle of the Humphrey Bogart movie *Casablanca*. Mae stepped over to Don and leaned in to his ear.

"You bring that girl here, young man," she said firmly.

"We'll do our best ma'am," Don said.

"We're that little lady's family now. We may be all she's got, but we'll sure enough be all she'll ever need. You bring that girl here."

"Praise Jesus," Aunt Lucy said.

"Hello?"

"Aaron? Don here."

"What'cha got for me, Captain?"

"I need you to write down a name."

"Hold on."

"I'll wait."

"Okay, give it to me."

164

"Sarah Wilkins. Write that down."

"Sarah Wilkins—got it."

"She's the lady I need you to find at the Methodist Mission in southern Little Rock."

"I know the mission, I know the church," Aaron said. "I said grace there a time or two. Went to a funeral at the church back in the forties."

"When you find her, this Sarah Wilkins, give her a message. Ready?"

"Ready."

"Tell her Aunt Lucy has arranged a taxi to come for your sister…"

"An…"

"No names, Aaron. Tell her Aunt Louise is coming to take her to Forrest City on Wednesday at five o'clock."

"Wednesday at five, got it."

"Tell her Aunt Lucy said it's important she be ready to go to keep the fare down."

"So, am I picking her up in my cab?"

"No, that's all taken care of. I don't want there to be any chance for you to get caught."

"It's because I'm…?"

"They're bad people, Aaron."

"You want some other guy to do it."

"Right."

"You mean…"

"Somebody who looks like them, the bad guys."

"I'm getting it now."

"They won't suspect the guy we pick will help her get away."

"I can dig it. What do I do?"

"Nothing yet. Just go about your normal activities, but not too far from a telephone. I'll get back to you."

"Okay."

"Can you go to the mission tonight and give Sarah Wilkins the message?"

"As soon as we hang up, I'll head there. I'll be back in an hour, maybe an hour and a half."

"There may be someone watching you talk with her. If you see any highway patrol, don't pay attention. Just tell her Aunt Lucy has a taxi coming to take the person to Forrest City on Wednesday at five o'clock. Be sure you use the words Aunt Lucy."

"I got it."

"She'll know it's code," Don said. "She'll know 'Aunt Lucy' is code that everything will be handled. Just tell her those words and leave. Don't hang around."

"I'm on my way."

Don let the earpiece hang down, clacking into the wall as it swung while he stepped to the table and opened his wallet. He picked paper notes and business cards from it. Leaving the wallet on the table, he took the cards back to the telephone and picked up the earpiece again. He cranked twice.

"Operator?"

"I need Conway 791 in Carlisle, Arkansas, on the line please."

"Busy night," Myrtie said.

While Myrtie was connecting the call, Don turned and looked at Jerry.

"Tall Jerry, where are your friends right now?"

"Some at the house, a bunch skating at Conway's. Why?"

"Not those friends. Where're Holbrook and Mary?"

"At the house. They're having spaghetti."

"Run home and pack a bag and tell them to pack and be ready. Pack warm—a heavy coat and your long johns."

"I will."

"What if their parents won't let them go?" Don asked.

"Oh, they can go."

166

"Why don't I drive Jerry to the falls," the doc said. "I can take Holbrook and Mary to their houses to pack."

"Perfect," Don said. "If we have to, can we meet up back here in your kitchen, Mae?"

"Of course, you can," Mae said. "You do whatever you have to and bring that girl here, where she'll be loved and nurtured."

Myrtie rang the number.

"Hoffman Dusters, Hal speaking," Hal Hoffman said.

"Connected," Myrtie said.

"Hold on, Hal," Don said.

He looked over and caught Jerry starting toward the door.

"Wait up a sec, Tall Jerry…don't leave until after this call."

He turned to the mouthpiece on the wall.

"Hal? It's Don."

"Why, hello, stranger, you proud poppa, you. How's the latest addition to that growing litter of yours?"

"Healthy baby," Don said. "Good looking, like his daddy."

"I'm lighting a cigar with your name on it on New Year's."

"Mary sends love to you and Janet and Happy Christmas. We're upstate in New York with Big Mike and Missus."

"Snowing there?"

"Snow on the ground, no snow tonight, but it's freezing," Don said.

"We got the Christmas card, Don. Why do I have honor of this long-distance call, my friend?"

"Hal, bear with me. I'm going to take you back a way."

"I'm not sure I…"

"It's important to me, Hal."

"Okay, I'll play your game."

"Do you remember Rheine?"

"Do I remember the Rhine?"

"Yes."

"The Rhine river in Germany?"

167

"No, the town Rheine in Germany."

"Hell yes, I remember that Rheine. How could I forget our first mission out?"

"That's the one."

"It was a predawn scramble. Remember that? Sirens going off every which way and all hell breaking out with us jumping out of our cots, pulling flight gear on and running about getting to our ships."

"Patton needed a precision-bomb attack on the bridges on the Dortmund-Ems-Kanal in Rheine to get ahead of two German tank divisions that were retreating and on their way to cross them," Don said.

"I remember we leveled them."

"We got them all," Don said.

"I think it was a thousand of us going out," Hal said. "Maybe more took off on that raid."

"That's it," Don said. "That's the morning I'm taking you back to. It was for the ground troops and tanks trying to win up the Battle of the Bulge."

"What brought this up, Don?"

"Something's come up and I thought about it."

"You getting nostalgic on me in your old age, buddy?"

"Aaron told me about your B-25 acquisition, Hal."

"I got two – one to fly, one for parts. She's sweet, Don."

"He tells me it's some special bird—a real lady in the sky."

"I can't wait for you to try her out. She's a beauty."

"So, how's he working out for you?"

"Aaron?"

"Yes."

"He's quite the mechanic. Great pilot, too. We're going to sell rides in her in the summer."

"Hal, what would you say if I told you I needed the loan of a B-25 for twenty-four, forty-eight hours this coming Wednesday?"

"You need a B-25?"

"I'd have it back sometime after Christmas."

"You need the loan of my B-25?"

"Yes, sir."

"You having some Christmas eggnog, are you, Don?"

"No."

"Into the early bubbly, are we?"

"I'm not drinking, Hal. Haven't had a drop."

"You're serious."

"I'm as serious as a heart attack. I need the B-25. Aaron told me all about it."

"So, it's a conspiracy between you two, eh," Hal said. "Dare I ask why you need it?"

"Something's come up. I was going to use a car, but I heard about your B-25. I'd like to leave it at that."

"Important to you, Don?"

"We might save a life."

"It's yours, my friend."

"Thanks, Hal."

"It's fueled and ready. If you need me, I'll be there, too."

"Best you clear out of there," Don said.

"When?"

"I wouldn't be around the airfield on Wednesday if you don't have to be. The less you know, the better."

"It's not much of an airfield, Don. A strip of mud when it rains. Dusters don't take much runway. This old turtle with wings takes its own sweet time thinking about liftoff."

"How's it looking now—the runway?"

"It's dry. You can get her up to speed."

"Like I say, if you don't need to be around Wednesday."

"Roger that," Hal said. "Wednesday I'll be home with the family, not here."

"Good."

"Don, it has almost the same cockpit configuration as our old B-17s. Do you think you can fly her?"

"Not sure, but I got the flying part and getting her up handled," Don said.

"I'm not even going to ask, but I can guess," Hal said. "He's good—he's really good."

Don looked at Allen, had an idea, and spoke into the phone for his benefit.

"Hal, none of my business, but can I ask how much Aaron costs—his flying and mechanical work? Is he a bargain?"

Allen looked up and waited to hear the answer. Hal was brief.

"For dusting, I gave him a choice of being the mechanic and keeping seventy percent of dusting fees after fuel when he flies or—"

Don repeated that so Allen could hear it.

"So, for flying the duster you give him a choice of either being the mechanic and keeping seventy percent of dusting fees after fuel when he flies or—"

"Or a straight dollar fifty an hour for everything," Hal said.

"Or a straight dollar fifty an hour for everything? That's a good wage," Don said.

"He's a good talent," Hal said.

"Merry Christmas, my friend," Don said.

"Oh, and Don," Hal said.

"I'm here."

"I'll leave my old sheepskin flight jumpsuit in the plane in case you need it."

Don smiled and hung up.

"Did you catch all that, Allen?"

Allen was wearing a most contented smile, because a brother was being treated fairly in the south.

Don pointed his finger at Jerry.

"It's your turn, Tall Jerry. Get your friend on the telephone."

170

He picked up the earpiece and held it out. Jerry cranked the phone twice.

"Operator?"

Myrtie, I need the Capital—"

"I know, the Capital Hotel in Little Rock, room 305."

"Yes."

"It sounds like you're up to something," Myrtie mumbled.

The connections became easier with each call to the hotel.

"Tall Jerry?" Hemingway asked.

"Yes, hi. We have more to the plan, I think."

"Let me have it."

Jerry held his hand over the mouthpiece and asked Aunt Lucy if she had the address of the Mission Methodist Church in southern Little Rock. She pulled the envelope from her purse. The address was in the upper left corner.

"Okay, write this address down," Jerry said.

He read the address to Hemingway and asked him to read it back. He had it perfect.

Don interrupted.

"Let me speak to him."

"Huh?" Jerry stuttered.

"Let me talk to him. Don't worry, I won't ask any questions."

Jerry told Hemingway to hold on for instructions and handed the earpiece to Don. Without saying "hello," Don started talking.

"Your passenger's name is Anna Kristina. She's expecting her cab at the Methodist Mission on Wednesday at five o'clock sharp. She'll be under the impression that you'll be taking her to the Forrest City Hospital, which would be about an hour-and-a-half drive."

"Anna Kristina, Methodist Mission, Wednesday, five o'clock sharp. Going to Forrest City Hospital—understood," Hemingway said.

"Make sure she's in the back seat."

"Good thinking," Hemingway said. "Gives less appearance of familiarity."

"Do you know Carlisle, Arkansas?" Don asked. "It's on the way to Forrest City but not far from Little Rock."

"I've passed through it, driving from Memphis," Hemingway said.

"There's a highway truck diner there—Red's Diner."

"Red's Diner. I remember seeing the flashing neon sign."

"Now this is important."

"I'm ready for important."

"Pull in to that diner like you have to go in and take a leak."

"Yes, sir."

"Park as far left as you can, next to the dirt drive beside the parking area."

"Far left, got it."

"The dirt drive goes behind the diner to an airfield."

"A private airport?" Hemingway asked.

"A take off and landing airstrip for crop dusters. Someone will be behind the trees there watching for you to drive up with the girl."

"This is brilliant."

"Get out of the car and go into the diner like nothing is happening."

"And the girl?" Hemingway asked.

"She's not allowed in the diner—that's what the sign on their door says," Don said. "So, you'll oblige them. She'll stay in the car. Remember to park as far to the left as you can, close to the dirt driveway next to the diner's west side."

"And I go inside?"

"Yes."

"And piss."

"We need you to stall for time."

"There's a chill in the air. It may be colder on Wednesday. Do I leave the car running?"

"Why not?"

"I just get out and go inside?"

"Yes, go inside, go to the men's room, and stall. Have a cup of coffee, a piece of pie."

"And here's where I'm not supposed to ask questions, right?"

"Don't lock the car doors," Don said.

"You the captain Tall Jerry speaks so highly of?" Hemingway asked.

"Actually, I was a lieutenant in the service. I'm a captain in the reserves now."

"Good job, Captain. Will there be any reason for me to stay around Little Rock?"

"No reason."

"If I think what's going to happen does happen, she won't be in my car when I come out and I can drive right to Memphis and catch a flight out?"

"Yes. If we pull it off, it'll happen fast."

"It's going to be my pleasure to serve under you, Captain."

"Thanks, mister. I don't know who you are, but thanks."

"When it's all over, Captain, ask my friend Tall Jerry. He will speak the truth."

Don handed Jerry the phone receiver.

"Good luck," Jerry said.

"Merry Christmas, my friend," Hemingway said. "Don't forget your New Year's research assignment."

"Remind me."

"The birds and the bees, my friend. The birds-and-bees talk."

"Oh, that. Yeah."

They both hung up.

"Tall Jerry," Don said. "How soon can you get your friends together for a meeting? We're going to need help on this end."

"This should be an SOS," Jerry said.

"How soon can they meet?"

"Most everybody is at Conway's, ice-skating. How about we set it for in the morning? Nine or ten?" Jerry asked.

"When are you going to want to fly, Don?" Big Mike asked.

"Wednesday," Don said. "If the highway patrol is out like you're saying they'll be, we don't want them to see any unnatural movement too early and give them the chance to react."

"The element of surprise," Mike Shea said.

"Bully!" the doc said.

"Ten, at the house," Big Mike said. "I'll have donuts."

"Ten works. I'll be better prepared," Don said.

"Are you going to tell Aaron?" Jerry asked.

"He's headed to Methodist mission now," Don said. "I'll call him later or in the morning before we meet."

Jerry ran outside with Doc. They headed off to the falls.

"Doc, you're driving Holbrook and Mary to their houses to pack a bag. Think you can bring them back? They should sleep at our house so none of us miss the meeting."

"Bully, young man. Bully! Count on me."

Big Mike, Mike Shea, and Allen were seeing the clear-headed thinking required to form battle strategies and tactics coming back to an experienced war veteran grappling with duty after duty without missing a detail. They sipped coffee with a pride a father would know.

Don turned the crank again and got the airline on the wire. He made reservations for four to fly from Syracuse to Memphis on Wednesday morning. He had one day to plan the trip.

He scribbled notes and pulled on his coat. He thanked the ladies for their patience and the puffballs. He tipped his hat.

"Gentlemen?" he asked Big Mike and Mike Shea.

He turned and shook Allen's hand.

"Best corned-beef hash I've ever had, Allen. I'll see you in a couple days for more, if you'll indulge me."

"You like pickled tongue?" Allen asked, standing up to say goodbye.

"I do indeed, with a stout bock," Don said. "Can't wait to try yours. Horseradish, too."

"Morning comes early for bakers and farmers," Big Mike said. "Thanks for the friendship and the coffee."

Allen smiled, involved in something that could change a life and maybe save one.

"Ladies?" Mike Shea asked. "We'll be off."

"What can Aunt Lucy and I do to help?" Mae asked.

"Just go about planning a good Christmas for your families, ladies," Mike Shea said. "Folks will be looking forward to a glorious midnight service, as always. That big tree out front of the church is quite a nice surprise this year."

"Mae, we'll drop Jackie and Alda back here," Big Mike said.

Mae had a tear in her eye.

"We're blessed having our girls grow up here, blessed."

They gave hugs, and left the Gaines's place, headed to the falls.

# CHAPTER 22

## PREFLIGHT PLANNING

Big Mike, Mike Shea, Allen and the doc were standing in the Delphi Falls kitchen with Missus and Mae, drinking coffee.

Must have been twenty people came early for the meeting. Cars dropped them off and then drove on back to farms to continue morning chores. As the kids walked in, they got a donut and a paper cup of hot chocolate and sat on the living room floor.

Don came out of a bedroom, rolling up his sleeves. He walked into the kitchen and poured a cup of coffee and stood by Big Mike and Aunt Mary. Mike Shea, Allen, and the doc had moved into the dining room.

"Listen up," Duba said.

Dick stepped up and stood next to the upright piano.

"How many of you know what's going on?"

Hands went up.

"So, we all know we're here to listen to the plan Don and Mr. Gaines have come up with. After that we'll see what we can do to help."

Don took a sip of his coffee, set the cup down on the counter and stepped over by the upright piano. "Tomorrow's the big day," he said.

Looking around, he decided to test the room.

"Who's in?"

Right arms in the room went up like a rocket.

"I grew up in Rochester," he began.

176

"Now I live in Little Rock, Arkansas. That's a long way away. Let me ask you a question. How many think I could have some friends in Rochester and some friends in Little Rock all at the same time?"

The crowd agreed it was likely.

"Well, to be safe on this mission we're about to go on, we have to assume that anybody we deal with in Arkansas might have connections up here."

Marty spoke up. "His point is simple. Loose lips sink ships. Whatever we learn today we keep to ourselves, or we could jeopardize the plan."

"He's right," Don said. "If the wrong ears hear it up here, they may tell people who know people in Little Rock, people in Arkansas that would want to stop us."

Dick stood. "Raise your right arms and repeat after me."

Arms went up.

"I pledge to keep what I hear secret, and I pledge I won't talk with anyone who's not in this room about it."

He looked around the room.

"If you pledge to do that, say, 'I pledge,'" Dick declared.

It was unanimous.

Don took over again.

"We're flying to Memphis, then we'll sneak into Arkansas."

"When?" Dick asked.

"Tomorrow. We're going to try to get the girl without anyone knowing and bring her to the Gaines's."

"Who's going?" Marty asked.

"Tall Jerry, Mary, and Holbrook are going. They decided."

"How do you get her out?" Dick asked.

Don didn't answer him.

"They can't fly her out," Duba said.

"Why not?" Marty asked.

"People at the airports will be watching the planes if the governor is involved in this," Big Mike said.

"No airports," Don said. "But let me keep that part of it secret. It'll be better that way."

"But we'll need fuel when we get here," he added. "Lots of fuel. By the time we get here we'll be on reserves."

With Don asking for fuel when they got here, you could have heard a pin drop. It was then the room knew for the first time that Don was going to fly a plane and that nobody would be on a passenger airline coming back.

"Regular gas or, airplane fuel?" Marty asked.

"Airplane fuel, full mix," Don said.

"There's Binghamton airport—that's on Route 11—or the Syracuse airport, Hancock Field," Big Mike said. "They'll both have fuel."

"If you land at those airports, tell us," Dick said. "We'll pick you up."

"We can't land at those," Don said. "We could be seen and get caught, at least on the way in."

"How will you get word to us if there's an emergency?" Dick asked.

"Good question," Don said. "Does anybody around here have a shortwave radio?"

"Myrtie does. Just call the New Woodstock operator, Myrtie," Duba said. "She'll pick up."

"For certain?"

"She'll pick up," Dick said. "She did it for civil defense in the war, and she does it for the sheriff in emergencies."

Don made notes in his spiral notebook.

"What's your plan?" Duba asked.

"We should have enough fuel to get here, land, and then takeoff to get to one of those airfields for fuel."

"I don't get it," Mayor said. "Can't you get caught just as easy if you go to an airport after you've come here?"

"I get it!" Marty said. "It won't matter by then if they don't have any passengers on board."

"And if we don't take off for a few days," Don said.

"Let the trail cool—get them off the scent," Holbrook said.

"That means you're going to have to land it around here some-where," Marty said. "Around Delphi Falls or somewhere near the hamlet."

"How much runway are you going to need?" Conway asked.

"For takeoff we'd need an even eight hundred feet loaded," Don said. "I'm thinking maybe five hundred feet with a lighter load."

"With a runway that long a body might think you're going to be flying a bomber," the doc said.

Don didn't flinch.

"The highway is out if it's a bomber," Conway said.

"The wings would be too wide and would catch fence posts or telephone poles," Barber said.

"Is that true?" Holbrook asked. "Are you going to fly a B-17?"

Don looked over at Allen and didn't answer.

"We'll need five or six hundred feet of runway," he repeated. "No roads."

"What direction will you be coming in from?" Conway asked. "I mean, once you get here. Will you be circling around?"

"Why would you need to know?" Don asked.

"If we know, we can tell you where you can land the fastest."

Don picked up his spiral notepad and looked at his notes.

"We'll be avoiding airports the best we can for as long as we can. We'll be flying from visual references to Chattanooga. From there, if the sky is clear, we'll follow the old US 11 all the way up here to Route 20."

"That's Cherry Valley," Barber shouted.

"If I remember my jigsaw-puzzle map of the United States of America," Marty said, "that means you're flying east then north, then turning south to land. Won't it burn more fuel, flying out of your way like that? That's a long trip."

"It's a precaution," Don said. "If we play our cards right, no one in Arkansas will suspect we're using a plane. But if we're seen, the more certain they are that we're headed due east, the better. They'll think we're going to Nashville or Charleston. They'll be thinking east, not north."

"Well then," Conway said. "Do you know Oran Delphi Road and where it crosses Route 20? We'll take you there and show you if you don't know."

"I know exactly where it is," Don said. "I went to Syracuse University after the war and drove it many times. It's at the foot—the lowest point—of the big hills between Pompey Center and Cazenovia," Don said.

"If you're following 11, hang east on 20 to Oran Delphi, and turn right, or south at that corner. You fly south until you see the car headlights on a field. We'll have six cars lined up with headlights on, marking the field on your left on Oran Delphi where you can land. It's Barber's field."

"Where will you be lined up with the cars?"

"I'm thinking side by side, so you'd know where the field is," Marty said.

"How about on the side of the field twenty feet apart so they can see more of the runway with our headlight beams?" Dick asked.

"Front end of the field would be better," Don said. If we can see the line of lights facing away down the field, we'll know to drop in from behind them and land in front of them. If it's too dark or fog is up, we'll know to come in from the north over them and trust there's enough runway to bring her to a full stop."

"Oh, you'll have enough runway," Barber said.

"What kind of field is it?" Don asked.

"It's a field," Barber said. "What do you mean, what kind?"

"What's it used for—corn, beans, or hay? It all makes a difference."

"Hay," Barber said.

"Why would that make a difference?" Randy asked.

"If the ground's been plowed and rough, it could break off our front wheel. We'd be able to land, but we'd keep the nose up until the last minute."

"It's hay. It's cut, too," Barber said.

"But we can't promise no woodchuck holes," Duba said.

"That's about it," Don said. "Takeoff will be at five o'clock—that's six Eastern Time. Little Rock is an hour earlier. We should be touching down here between ten and eleven, depending on winds."

"We'll be there to pick you up," Dick said.

"There'll be tarps in the plane," Don said. "We could use help covering the engines."

"Those with cars or tractors who can do the runway duty tomorrow, meet up at my place after milking today. We'll go see what the field looks like in the dark and mark our posts."

"Thanks for being here, everybody," Don said.

He stepped back into the kitchen.

## CHAPTER 23

## LAST CHANCE TO CHICKEN OUT

Mary and Holbrook slept over, but none of them had a good night's sleep. Instead they were thinking about trouble they might get into going to Little Rock. Missus had Wheaties in bowls waiting for them on the table, along with milk and sugar and spoons.

"There's no Christmas tree here, Jerry. Don't you guys put up a tree?" Mary asked.

"Santa brings our tree," Jerry said.

"That's nice," Mary said.

They stood at the kitchen counter, munched their Wheaties, waiting for Don to appear and to tell them what to do. Big Mike came in the side door, through the laundry room. He was dressed in his suit, tie, and overcoat. He had been to the bakery in Homer and back.

"Don's outside. Finish your breakfast, and we'll go."

"Are you going with us?" Holbrook asked.

"I'm taking you to the airport."

Holbrook and Jerry grabbed coats from a chair and began stuffing things in a knapsack. Mary had a small suitcase already packed resting on the piano bench in the living room. Big Mike saw the bags and reminded them that they would be coming home tonight and wouldn't need all those things. They hung onto their winter coats and walked out to the car.

"If you have gloves or mittens, I'd get them," Don said.

Missus went through a box in the front hall closet and found gloves and winter hats that fit each of them.

182

Mary, Holbrook, and Jerry sat in the back seat. Snow flurries started to dance in the swirling wind. It didn't appear to be wet snow. Big Mike drove, and Don sat in the passenger seat, turning pages in his small spiral notepad. Holbrook had never flown, and Big Mike suggested they get him a barf bag from behind the seat in the plane in case he needed it. Mary had been up with Flying Eddie in his biplane. She was fine with flying. Jerry was, too.

Big Mike pulled up to the airport terminal. "They predict this snow is going to build," he said. "Will it be a problem?"

"In all my missions, there was never a weather option. If the Allies had become weather dependent, Hitler would have known when we'd attack and when we'd dig in just by watching the weather reports. We had to take off in any weather."

Don turned in his seat and looked at his team, one at a time.

"If any of you want to change your mind, now's the time. I won't mind if any of you choose to stay."

None of them so much as blinked. They were ready.

"So," Don said. "Listen carefully."

He turned around and knelt in the front seat with his back leaning on the dashboard.

"Do you remember what I told your friends about my growing up in Rochester, and now I'm living in Little Rock, and how easy it would be for me to know people in both areas?"

"We remember," Mary said.

"I want you to know that passengers on the airplane today will be just like that. They're coming from here, Syracuse, and will be flying to Memphis with us. Think they'll know people in both cities?"

"Probably," Jerry said.

"Isn't Memphis in another state?" Mary asked. "We're going to Arkansas."

"Memphis is on the Mississippi border of Arkansas not far from Little Rock."

"Oh," Mary said.

"Best way to spill a secret is to talk," Don said. "Best way to not talk is to sleep."

"What?" Mary asked.

She stuck out her lip and puffed a curl from her eye.

"Can't I just look out the window?" Holbrook asked.

"Look all you want. Just don't get into conversations with anyone and risk spilling the beans. The few hours we'll be there will be critical, and we don't want to be sending out advance signals to anyone."

"What if somebody asks me why I'm flying to Memphis?" Mary asked.

"Here's a trick," Don said. "Just say the word *Christmas* if anybody asks you anything. Just say one word, *Christmas.*"

"Okay," Jerry said. "*Christmas.* I can do that."

"Most people know kids are taught not to talk with strangers. If you just say *Christmas*, they'll be good with that. Say it and go on your way."

"Anything else we should know?" Mary asked.

"Mary, I didn't want to tell you too far in advance. I didn't want you to worry."

"Tell me what?"

"The girl we're going to get is pretty far along."

"I know she's pregnant. Aunt Lucy told me all about it."

"Well, there's more to it, Mary."

"Like what?"

"We think she's due this month. I need you to stay close to her and keep calm. She's young and should listen to you. Keep reminding her that you're Aunt Lucy's friend."

"I can do that. Don't worry."

"Anything else?" Jerry asked.

"Try not to talk with one another until we get there, in case someone can overhear."

"Is that like flying on radio silence, Don?" Holbrook asked. "Like in *Thirty Seconds Over Tokyo* with Spencer Tracy?"

"Exactly," Don said.

"Wow. This is good!" Jerry said.

"Try to sleep. We have a lot to do when we get down there and not much time to do it," Don said. "After we land just stick close to me, try to keep up, and listen for my instructions."

"Don," Mary said. "I promise we won't disappoint you."

"Let's go," he said.

Big Mike gave them a thumbs-up as they climbed out, forming a single-file line following Don to the airline counter, where a lady handed him their tickets. They walked down a sidewalk and onto the airplane, where a stewardess in a blue suit and a hat welcomed them on board. They found a row that had two seats on either side of the aisle. Don pointed to one and let Mary sit next to a window, and he sat beside her. Holbrook was next to the window on the other side, and Tall Jerry sat in the aisle seat next to him.

"Buckle up," Don said.

The two engines out Holbrook's window belched smoke and propellers began to spin. The airplane taxied down the runway with the roar of engines, and they were in the air. Holbrook gasped with delight at the sudden sensation of weightlessness.

Don woke them up in Memphis after the airplane touched down. It stopped and the engines were turned off.

They followed him like goslings. They walked at a normal pace to not attract attention. Don would look around to see if they were all with him. They walked past a bale of cotton by the side door and through the airline terminal. There was a Christmas tree in the middle of the terminal and decorations on the walls. They didn't stop for anything. Don walked through the building and out the front door. Without skipping a beat, they found their way to the second row of cars in the parking lot and passed in front of a Buick with a Tennessee plate on it, an Oldsmobile with a Mississippi plate, and an old Plymouth with a plate so muddy they couldn't read it.

Don pointed to a Chevrolet to the left of a Plymouth. Through the window he could see Aaron, Anna Kristina's brother, the man he and Jerry had met on Thanksgiving. He was sitting behind the wheel.

Don turned about, searching for people who might have been watching. He saw no one.

"Holbrook!" he said in a loud whisper. "Get in the front and crouch down on the floor and stay down."

He stepped to the back door and opened it.

"Mary, jump in the back and slide over, but sit on the seat. Tall Jerry, you get in the back and crouch on the floor in front of her and stay down."

They moved like they trusted Don implicitly and assumed he and the driver of the car had it all planned out. No one said a word.

The car started and pulled away. Holbrook and Jerry on the floor could tell when they stopped at a stoplight and which way they were turning when they turned. It wasn't long before they looked up from the floor and out through the rear window and saw the steel girders of a bridge they were driving over. Just before they drove off the end of the bridge on the other side, Don started to talk.

"Okay, stay down until we get there," he said. "Don't get up off the floor, but this is Aaron. Aaron is my friend and is helping us."

"Hello," Aaron said. "God bless you."

Jerry tapped Don on the leg to get his attention, and then he pointed at his mouth to see if he could talk.

"You can talk. Just stay down until we get there," Don said.

"Hi, Aaron, remember me?" Jerry asked.

"I remember you, young man. God bless you for coming."

"Was that the Mississippi River we went over?" Jerry asked.

"The mighty Mississippi, it surely was," Aaron said. "Welcome to Arkansas, everybody."

"Why are we on the floor?" Holbrook asked.

"A car full of people is looked at by the authorities if there's suspicion of foul play. They're suspicious of what may look like a gang. A man and his daughter with a driver in a taxi wouldn't draw attention."

"Especially if the car is coming into Arkansas, and they aren't trying to skip out," Aaron added with a grin.

"When will we be there?" Mary asked.

"Carlisle is one hundred and six miles from Memphis," Don said. "We should be there by three o'clock. That'll give us a couple of hours to walk through it and to get ready."

There was silence most of the way.

Close to three the car slowed and pulled off the highway, not coming to a stop. In a crawl, it turned right on what felt and sounded like the gravel driveway in Delphi Falls.

"Don, if you jump out and get the hangar door, I'll pull in," Aaron said. "It takes a good yank, but it'll lift."

"Stay put until we're inside with the door closed," Don said.

He got out of the car, pulled the strap and the overhead door rolled up. It was still climbing as the car made its way into the dark hangar and stopped beside an enormous B-25 bomber in army green with a star on its tail. Aaron stepped out of the car, walked over to the doorway and looked outside to see if anyone was watching. With a heave on its chain, the entrance door came back down, putting them in darkness. There was a sharp clunk of a breaker switch, and four bulbs inside the hangar came on.

"You all can get out now," Don said.

The Mary, Tall Jerry, and Holbrook stood under the wing of the bomber in awe, staring up at the plane that had made history during the war.

"Look at how big the engines are, though," Tall Jerry said.

"I thought it would be bigger," Holbrook said.

"It's a medium bomber, son," Don said.

"Designed with speed in mind for quick drops and fast turn-arounds and used more for air cover than for strategic bombing like the big boys, the B-17s or the B-29s," Aaron said.

"Aaron, can you open the bomb-bay doors for loading?" Don asked.

"Will do."

"Tall Jerry and Holbrook," Don said. "There's a mattress rolled up and tied with some rope somewhere in this warehouse. Find it and lift it up into the cargo hole of the plane. Then find four tarps somewhere."

"They's over by the office," Aaron said.

"Over by the office," Don said. "Get them loaded up."

"Keep the tarps rolled," Aaron said. "They's all the seats we'll have back there. Y'all will need them to sit on. Roll them tight."

"What can I do?" Mary asked.

Don pulled a pamphlet from his coat pocket. It was a pamphlet from Dr. Brudney. He handed it to her.

"Read this. It's about all the signs to look for when someone is close to having a baby."

Mary looked up in a blank stare.

"Just read it," Don said.

Then he turned about.

"Let's go, folks. Put a move on. Get done and we'll tell you what's next."

Don waited for Aaron to drop the bomb-bay doors and climb down from the plane. He and Aaron stepped around in front of the B-25.

"What's the plan, Aaron? She's your bird."

"Huh?" Aaron asked. "You're flying her, Captain. Ain't that the plan?"

"Now why would I want to be flying your plane?" Don asked. "Besides, it's a ship I'm not checked out on. No way am I flying it, especially with a talent as good as you standing in the same hangar."

Don stood at attention and snapped a salute.

"Awaiting orders, Captain!" he said.

"You mean…?" Aaron started.

Don held his salute without so much as a smirk. He was dead serious. Aaron stood tall, returning the salute. It was a salute he'd been waiting to return since 1942. It was a salute of respect from Captain Don, seasoned veteran with thirty-three missions into Hitler's hellhole behind him. That meant something to Aaron—it truly did. That was important to him. He didn't waste a moment on tears.

"Anna Kristina is being picked up at five o'clock," Aaron said. "That means that between five fifteen and five thirty, a car should be pulling into the diner's parking lot."

Aaron looked at his wristwatch.

"Set our watches to three twenty-two," Aaron said. "In an hour, at four thirty, I want to do the full walk-through and preflight check of this lady while she's in the hangar. She'll be ready to fly before we pull her out."

He handed Don a checklist sheet a B-25 had to go through before takeoff.

"After preflight we'll open the doors, rev her high, and taxi quick down next to a clump of pine trees by the rice silos behind the diner. That'll hide the plane from view. If anyone should see us while we're taxiing, they'll think we've taken off and are long gone. It'll also be chocked close enough to the trees so getting the girl from the car on board won't be too far a walk. She'll be scared enough without adding a hike to the other end of the runway."

"Sounds like a plan," Don said. "You'll have the ship revved and ready to bust loose for takeoff. I'll bring the girl from the car and get her on board."

"No disrespect, Captain, but that's a negative," Aaron said. "I'll go get the girl. She's my sister. She may not know my face, but for sure the last thing the girl will be trusting tonight is yours. I'll be getting her on board. Then I'll pull the chocks and throw them in. You be in that left seat and ready to take off when we're boarded, and we won't look back."

"Yes, sir," Don said with a salute. "Where's the wind likely to be coming from this time of day?"

"That's the bad news, now ain't it?" Aaron asked. "It'll most likely be a tail wind coming from that end of the runway. The wind will be with you and a harder takeoff, but I figured it'll be safer if no one's able to see the plane startin' up or takin' off. To do that, we have to take off from the wrong end of the runway."

"You give me a good cockpit tour, and I'll get her up," Don said. "We're not carrying guns, bombs, or ammo. We should be light enough to do a Doolittle." (Don referred to Jimmy Doolittle's B-25s taking off from the short aircraft carrier to bomb Tokyo in 1942.)

"Get her up, do a hard bank starboard around and point her to Chattanooga," Aaron said.

"Count on it," Don said. "Then you'll take over from there, Captain. The left seat is yours on this mission."

Aaron pursed his lips; gave a shy, proud twist of his head; looked up at the B-25 cockpit's front window with a twinkle in his eye; and then twinkled another look over to the clock on the wall in the back of the hangar. He was savoring the moment for himself, feeling every second of it, and locking into memory how it felt and what it was like to be looked at and treated as an equal.

"Where's the coffee urn?" Don asked. "Let's get some joe and then you can give me a walk-through of this great lady, Captain."

"Over in the office," Aaron said. "Follow me, but we're out of sugar."

# CHAPTER 24

## ALL SYSTEMS GO

Aaron climbed into the pilot's seat, preparing to taxi the plane partway down the dirt runway into hiding. Don was waiting below to close the hangar door after he pulled out. Holbrook, Mary, and Tall Jerry were on board, sitting in the dark. The shaking screech of the engines cranking up one at a time inside the tin hangar was deafening. Each engine prop turned slowly at first and then seemed to gasp for air, and suddenly burst into a spin. They held their ears but kept their eyes open, looking for signals or instruction. Aaron was waiting for Don's signal that the coast was clear for the taxi out of the hangar. He turned his head about and shouted back.

"I'd put your coats on if I were you. It'll be cold back there."

Holbrook gave him a thumbs-up as the engine's RPMs increased, revving up into high decibels. Don waved an all-clear signal with his handkerchief, and the B-25's front wheel hopped up as the brakes were released, and she started to roll out of the hangar. Outside Aaron pushed on the brakes, and it came to a rocking stop while Don pulled the hangar overhead closed. Holbrook and Jerry moved about and lowered the boarding ladder from the belly of the plane. Don padlocked the hangar door, walked underneath the plane and climbed up and in. Aaron waited for them to pull the ladder up and lock it. He released the brakes while still at a high rev, and the plane jolted forward, picking up a convincing takeoff speed. They rolled down the runway to the clump of pine trees and the rice silos behind the diner. Just past the trees and out of sight, he stepped on the right brake, causing the plane to swing about sharply as he

191

lowered the revs, turning it almost in a 360 turn. He brought it to a full stop and quickly shut down the two engines. The silence with the engines off caused a vacuum in the back.

Don pointed a finger at Jerry until he had his attention.

"You're the only one here who knows what your friend looks like. Think you can get to the other side of those pine trees over there without being seen and watch for him?"

Holbrook and Jerry had played this game a million times in the woods over Delphi Falls. They were good at stealth. They could stalk a crow without being seen.

"I can do it," Jerry said.

"The second you see him, run back here and tell us."

Don looked at his watch. He looked up to the front of the B-25 and caught Aaron's eye.

"Ready in seventeen!" Don barked.

Aaron looked at his watch and computed seventeen minutes from that second. He climbed out from the pilot's seat, crawled back, sat on a tarp next to Holbrook. Then he took his leather-and-sheepskin flight suit from a bag and rolled it out on the floor.

Don lowered the bomb-bay doors, all the time keeping his eyes on his wristwatch. At the proper moment he pointed to Jerry to get ready. He clicked his finger.

"Now!" he said.

Jerry didn't wait. He rolled onto his stomach and hung his legs down the bomb-bay opening, ready to drop himself to the ground. Don had intended for him to climb down the boarding ladder, but he grabbed his wrist, and they locked together as he leaned out from the plane and lowered Jerry down far enough so he could drop without getting hurt.

"Go! " Don said.

Jerry took off running and Aaron started lowering a ladder to the ground carefully, not letting it fall. Entering through the bomb-bay doors would be easier for the pregnant girl than entering on the boarding ladder. Aaron crawled over and sat in the bomb-bay door opening with his feet hanging over it, holding the ladder post. He was waiting for the signal from Jerry that the car with his sister in it had pulled in. Mary lowered her head through the opening, watching for the signal. Don climbed into the pilot's seat, examining his takeoff-checklist sheet, flipping switches in anticipation. He tightened a comfort grip on the wheel and looked about the pilot's cabin. He turned his head.

"Holbrook and Mary," he shouted. "When the bomb-bay door is closed and locked, open the mattress flat. There should be two blankets inside. After the girl is on board, try to make her comfortable. You may have to hang on to her and roll the mattress in half over her to keep her from bouncing around during takeoff. We'll be lifting off right away. Watch your footing."

The mission started up like a train car full of fireworks busting loose. Tall Jerry saw Ernest Hemingway driving in with a girl in the back seat. Jerry turned and bolted back to the B-25, waving his arms to signal to them.

"They're here!" Jerry shouted.

"They're here!" Mary yelled, relaying his signal.

Jerry reached the plane and looked up through the bomb-bay doors.

"They just pulled in," Jerry shouted up.

"Stay where you are," Aaron said. "I'm coming down."

Aaron stepped onto the ladder and lowered himself to the ground. As he stepped away from the plane, he looked at Jerry and said, "Tall Jerry, you have to stand still. Hold the ladder, and don't move a muscle while he starts the engines. It's very dangerous, the props and all. You cannot move one inch from this ladder. Do you understand me?"

"Yes, sir," Jerry said. "I understand."

"Good. Now, when your friend comes down the ladder, you tell him the same thing."

"Will do," Jerry said.

Aaron looked up and shouted, "Don! Can you hear me?"

"Loud and clear," Don shouted."

"We're all clear!" Aaron shouted.

"Roger that," Don said.

Aaron turned like an infantryman and walked at a good pace through the trees, disappearing around the side of the rice silos. The second he was out of sight, Don turned a switch to start the left engine. It whined a shrill and whined again until it belched a billow of black smoke, and then the engine caught and whirred the propeller at a high rev. He turned his head and shouted for Holbrook.

"Holbrook, time for you to climb down and get ready to help the girl get on board! Mary, can you hear me?"

"I can hear you!" Mary shouted.

"Once she's on board, get her settled because we'll be rolling and taking off just as soon as we get the doors locked!"

"I will! I'll take care of her!" Mary shouted.

The right engine started turning. It busted and popped, coughed and stalled out. It stirred again, this time sounding a familiar whine, turning until it puffed black smoke, and the propeller chomped and instantly spun free, ready to fly.

Jerry hung onto the ladder while Aaron and the girl came around the rice silos, circling behind the trees. Aaron had his arm around her, helping her from tripping in the turf. He was holding her coat and a pillowcase with all her belongings. Anna Kristina was carrying her baby low in her belly, her clothes didn't fit well, and her eyes were as big as quarters, filled with trepidation and fear. The only thing she trusted, perhaps, was her brother, Aaron, but ole Charlie here knew that her first thought about him was that she wasn't certain he hadn't sold the lot out to get on somebody's good side.

As they walked, not a word was spoken between them. Anna Kristina didn't show any fear of climbing the ladder or any sign that she needed help. Mary was at the top with a smile, and she helped the girl over to the mattress. Aaron sent Holbrook and Jerry up the ladder next. He was last to climb in. He paused just as his head was at the top rung and looked back to see if they had been seen. The Christmas Eve, it seemed, was in their favor. Not a creature was stirring.

He lifted the ladder and raised the bomb-bay doors and locked them.

"All aboard and secure, Captain," he shouted.

The engines had been at the highest rev for the past minute or two in anticipation of takeoff. Don lifted both feet from the brakes and pressed on one, and the B-25 lunged forward, turning about and heading to the base of the runway. Without pause, Don stomped the alternate brake pedal to turn the plane again, and it pulled around in a half circle, the engines revving. And like a frog, it leaped forward.

Just as he had done on thirty-three missions, Don counted to himself: "Five seconds, ten seconds." He could feel it in his fingers. The hangar in the background was coming closer—closer. "Fifteen seconds." And then, "It's time, sweetheart," he mumbled through clenched teeth.

Don arm-wrestled the wheel back, showing no weakness. And in twenty-four seconds, they lifted off the ground.

"Grab something and hang on!" Aaron yelled.

The B-25 had lifted to maybe two thousand feet when, without warning, it rolled nearly on its side into a starboard bank to turn right and right again until they were heading due east. Don, looking down during takeoff, could see cars in the diner's parking lot, two regular cars and one state highway patrol car with the trooper 'bubble' light on its roof.

Aaron grabbed the sheepskin flight suit and began to pull it on. He turned a flashlight on and crawled on his hands and knees over to the mattress. He paused and stared into Anna Kristina's eyes. She was beyond fright. She had no more despair to give. She had been through a lot for a sixteen-year-old girl. All she had then was the comfort of Mary's warm hand and a promise that Aunt Lucy, who she'd never met, was at the other end of this nightmare. She looked at Aaron. She wanted to believe his eyes. She wanted him not to be a stranger. He took her other hand.

"Don't be afraid, Anna Kristina," he said. "No need to be afraid ever again."

"I'm not afraid," she said. "I'm scared, but I'm not afraid."

It seemed in her reserve she showed he would have to earn her trust. He had abandoned her all these years. She was happy to see her brother for the first time she could ever recall. It seemed she wasn't put off by not having been family with him for all that time. Anna Kristina had grown up in a culture of people who could still remember slavery as their heritage, a culture of people who'd had members of their families sold off and separated from them—who'd had no rights to do anything about it other than pray to God or sing to the soul or to all their own kin, no matter where they were. But he wasn't taken from her. He left her life on his own. He would have to earn her trust. This night was a good start.

Aaron crawled into the front cockpit. Don turned and saluted, unbuckled his seat belt and shoulder-harness straps, and gave him the left seat—and with it, full command of the B-25. Don took the right seat.

*Don after saluting Captain Aaron.*

"Tall Jerry!" he shouted back.

Jerry made his way up to the cockpit's opening.

"Yes?" he asked.

"There're two footlocker boxes back there," Don said. "One has a bucket and two relief tubes in it. The other has sandwiches and soda pop."

"Okay," Jerry said.

"If anyone has to go, tell them to use the bucket or the relief tubes," Don said.

"Huh?" Jerry asked.

"You'll figure it out. Show the two lockers to Mary."

The plane seemed to settle down, rolling less, and flying more smoothly than it had during takeoff from the dirt field. It was plowing along through the clouds in a darkening sky at ten thousand feet.

With Aaron in control, Don opened a map, examined it and folded it down to the area he was interested in studying.

"I'm reckoning an hour and a half to Chattanooga," he said.

"That feels about right," Aaron said.

"Then set heading one-fifty degrees north to Binghamton, and then we set a heading zero-one-zero degrees to our destination. We'll use visual references to bring her in."

"What's the field look like?" Aaron asked.

"That's just it," Don said. "It's a field on a farm near Delphi Falls. I figured it's safer that way—not a commercial airfield and out of sight. It should be frozen and not muddy. If the winds are with us, we'll have a hundred or so mile reserve fuel to get us to Binghamton to fuel up for return."

"This lady loves to fly," Aaron said. "She's looking forward to stretching her wings. With a little luck, we'll bring her in jus' fine."

"We're lucky you're the captain," Don said.

Aaron beamed a toothy, childlike grin. "Me? How's that?"

"We couldn't be any luckier than this," Don said. "We have a top-rate medium-bomber pilot who trained in freezing-cold Michigan winters flying us into what I think may be some weather when we get there."

"Full moon tonight," Aaron said. "Good nighttime visuals in the snow under a full moon."

*Aaron returns salute and takes command.*

# CHAPTER 25

## SNOW STORMS AND FEARS

Don looked down and had a visual reckoning of Chattanooga, Tennessee below. He signaled their position and Aaron banked the B-25 onto 150 degrees bearing north to Binghamton, putting the setting sun on his portside window.

At that same moment, up at Barber's farm near the Delphi hamlet, the telephone rang.

"Hello?"

"Mrs. Barber, this is Conway. Is Barber there?"

"He's just come in from shoveling snow. Hang on, dear."

"Hello?"

"Barber, the radio said this is going to be a record snowfall. No letup in sight until after dark."

"It's not looking good," Barber said.

"The worst since '49," Conway said.

"Dad says with the wind, it could drift six, eight feet," Barber said.

"We only have a couple hours before dark and they'll be here needing that field to land," Conway said.

"If we're going to do something we have to move fast," Barber said.

"Can you set up a meeting?" Conway asked. "Your place would be fastest."

"Set up a meeting with who? Tall Jerry, Holbrook, and Mary aren't even here."

"Get anybody who can come."

"It's Christmas Eve."

"I know, and it'll be tough finding people. For sure get Randy and his pap if you can find them. Try Bases, Mayor, Marty, Dwyer, Duba, Dick."

"How about Sheriff John Price, if I can find him?"

"Him, too."

"I'll try."

"Any others who can get rides to your place through the snow and wind?"

"Do you want Judy Clancy, Alda, and Jackie?"

"They're having choir practice at the church for tonight's service—if they're still having one. Let's leave them there."

"The hayfield they're supposed to be landing on is a real mess," Barber said.

How bad?" Conway asked.

"I'll bet there's two feet on it already. We never got the snow fence up. It's drifting across Oran Delphi and piling up in the field."

"No way they'll be able to land there."

"Not if we don't put a move on, they won't," Barber said.

"Make your calls! Set it up right away. I'm hanging up and heading out the door. I'll be down to your place with the tractor and plow. We've got to get that field cleared or somebody will get hurt."

"I'll make the calls."

"Wait," Conway said. "How about trying Mike Shea, Big Mike, and the doc?"

"Mr. Gaines, too?" Barber asked.

"Give it a shot. We've nothing to lose asking. I'll see ya when I see ya."

*Click.*

Mrs. Barber was a woman with a ready smile and a stern disposition. She had to be strong, cooking for and feeding a room filled with farm hands breakfast at five in the morning and dinner at twelve o'clock noon. She was Mrs. Clause this night, with her hand-sewn, Christmassy red apron, a sprig of holly safety-pinned to its front. She had the fireplace crackling ablaze and had stacked a pile of firewood at its side. The huge, round dining room table had been cleared of salt and pepper shakers for the meeting. She was in the kitchen warming cider in a soup caldron and had a passel of mugs and a stack of cinnamon sticks on the dining room table ready to go with the cider for the young ones. There was a jug of rum for the older folks in case they favored a Christmas nip in their cider to cut the chill.

Thanks to the doc's Jeep and Mr. Vaas's milk-can-hauler rig, the dining-room gathering around that table was ample to get through this and get the job done before the plane showed up. The adults there were Mike Shea, Doc Webb, Big Mike, Allen Gaines, Mr. Barber, and Mr. Vaas. Among my flock included Conway, Duba, Dick, Dwyer, Mayor, Randy Vaas, Bases, Barber, and Marty Bays. Most Barber tried to call were at their grandparents' homes for Christmas or outside shoveling snow and not able to hear telephones ring. Just as the meeting was about to start, Sheriff John Price opened the side door. He stomped his feet on the mat, shaking snow from his hat before he walked in.

"How'd you make it here, Sheriff John?" Mike Shea asked. "The roads like they are?"

"Tire chains and a bag of sand in the trunk, just in case."

Mrs. Barber came in and set her big caldron down on the edge of the table with a gentle clunk. She ladled cider from it and slid one tall mug at a time for the nearest to grab and slide it to the next, who would in turn pass it on until everyone had a mug warming his hands.

Conway stood. "I called Farmer Parker. He said we can use his horses if we need them."

"Sarge and Sally," Marty said. "I've worked with them."

"Marty, you know horses better than most," Mr. Barber said. "How long would it take to get a team from Parker's over to here?"

"Hard to say, in this weather," Marty said. "On dry ground with a load, a team can travel about five miles per hour."

"You learn this farming or in school, Marty?" Big Mike asked.

"I told you the boy knew his way around a horse," Mr. Barber said.

"Tell you, though," Marty said. "After I harness 'em up I'll be riding on the back of old Sarge and steering them both. I may get more speed without a haul. Given we still have some daylight left, maybe a half hour over here, it'll be dark. Once I get them through the hamlet, even if it's dark, I'll get an eyeball on your house lights and follow that."

"That may work," Mike Shea said.

"Trick is," Marty said. "How are you going to get me over to Farmer Parker's?"

Marty was smart, or did ole Charlie here tell you that already?

"Well we had to come in my Jeep," the doc said.

"The roads are getting worse," Big Mike said.

"Big Mike got his Olds stuck in a snow bank at our place," the doc said. "My Jeep is all that would make it up Reynolds' hill to get Mike Shea. In a couple hours, the roads may not be passable, even with my Jeep."

"It's not letting up, folks," Sheriff John said.

"I think I speak for the elders here," Big Mike said. "They've already been in the air an hour or so. Tell us what you need from us, and we'll all give it our best and try to help you make it happen."

"Hear, hear!" the doc said.

"Well first things first," Conway said. "We need to clear an airstrip on that hayfield."

"Did you bring your tractor and plow?" Barber asked.

"She's out front," Conway said.

"Well that handles the snowplowing," Mayor said.

"But we promised Don car headlight beams at the bottom end of the runway, so they could see the field," Conway said. "There ain't no way we're going to get eight or ten cars down there and on the field in this snow."

"Ain't no way," Mayor repeated.

"With no cars and no headlight beams, there's no sense even plowing if they can't see the field to land on it," Mr. Vaas said.

The doc stood and stepped around the table and out into the kitchen.

With him stepping out of the room, Conway felt he was losing control of the meeting.

"I guess besides the doc's Jeep, maybe Sheriff John's car and our Moline tractor are the only things that can get through. And if there are no lights on the landing strip, what good would a plowed field be?"

"I just said that," Mayor said.

Mumblings and grumblings started to take over the room. Opinions and thoughts were being bantered about with or without thought. It was during some back and forth on the topic of head-lights on the landing strip that the doc came back into the room with a broad Teddy Roosevelt smile on his face. He stepped to the side of Mrs. Barber, picked up the rum keg, admired the fireplace and flavored his cider. He passed the keg over to Mike Shea. While still standing, he let out a bark that quieted the room.

"Barber!?" the doc bellowed.

That room got so quiet you could hear a kitten's purr.

"Do you have a wagon around here that'll hitch to Conway's Minneapolis Moline tractor?"

Mr. Barber answered for young Barber. "We have two," he said. "One's a flat-bedded hay wagon, and the other's a buckboard rigged for pulling with a tractor. We use it for hauling wire for fencing."

"Let's get them both hitched up."

"What for?" Mr. Barber asked.

"I just called ole man Moore…You all know Moore from the apple farm up across Cherry Valley on Pompey Hollow Road."

"Judy and I've been there for apple festival," Conway said. "Everybody knows it."

"We know the Moores," Mr. Barber said.

"Mr. Moore just happens to have spares and is going to lend us eight smudge pots we can use for light on the airstrip."

"Smudge pots?" Mike Shea asked.

"They're oil-filled and will burn all night in a blizzard if they need to," the doc said.

"Good thinking, Doc," Allen said. "Mighty good thinking."

"But you'll have to go get them," the doc said.

"An airplane would be able to see smudge pots from the air for miles," Marty said.

"I'll see if Myrtie can keep her shortwave tuned in," Sheriff John said. "Just in case they try to call in from the plane."

"How bad will the roads be when they get close, say, two or three hours from now?" Marty asked.

"Unpassable, most likely," Sheriff John said.

By this time the room had broken into warm cider–inspired mutterings, some rum speculating *what ifs*, and a number of other dysfunctional, go-nowhere utterances when Mrs. Barber walked in the room with a refilled caldron of warm cider and began rapping on the dining room table with her tin cider ladle.

*Crack, crack, crack, crack.*

The room came to a respectful silence.

"Here you are!" she said.

"What's on your mind, Gertie?" Mr. Barber asked.

"Here you are, grown men blabbing away like old hens at a tea-party social while a frightened little sixteen-year-old pregnant girl is flying in the freezing cold somewhere between us and God."

"Why, Gertrude we were just—" Mr. Vaas started.

"I know what you were doing. You were all just circling the wagons and not thinking clear," she bellowed.

She then paused and waited for any signs of intelligent life among those at the table. Other than Conway, who was speechless but sitting there with his mouth open like he was about to say something, she found none. This was when Mrs. Barber and her ladle officially took charge.

"So, the roads will be impassable, will they Sheriff John?" Mrs. Barber asked.

"They will be," Sheriff John said.

"And just where is the girl supposed to be going when she gets here?"

"Our place," Allen said.

"Could your tractor get through to the Gaines's place, Jimmy?" Mrs. Barber asked. "Could it get through from the airstrip down Oran Delphi all the way over to the Gaines's place?"

"Not after hours of snow buildup and wind—not without plowing, which could take hours," Conway said.

Mrs. Barber raised her fist that was grasping the ladle, rested the back of her hand under her chin in thought, and looked over at Marty.

"Could horses get through, Marty?"

"If they could see, they could. They can see in the dark, but blinded by snow, probably not," Marty said.

"Wagon wheels wouldn't make it either," Mayor said.

Mumbles in the room began to mutter again. Once again Mrs. Barber cracked the ladle on the table.

*Crack, crack, crack, crack.*

"Marty!" she barked. "You ride in the doc's Jeep with Big Mike and Mike Shea. Doc, you drop Marty at Farmer Parker's."

"Can do," the doc said.

"Marty, when you get there, harness up Farmer Parker's horses and get back here while the roads are passable and the horses aren't snow-blinded and you can still see."

"Why here, Mom?" Barber asked.

206

"The straw loft of the old feed barn, son."

"Huh?" Barber grunted.

"There's a horse-drawn sled with benches up there in that loft, hanging on the wall," Mrs. Barber said. "It'll carry four or five easy. A couple of you lugs go help get it down. Get her rigged up for a team of horses. You might grease the runners. If wheels won't make it through the snow, by golly that sleigh surely will."

That room caught a stillness from stirring and mouth jabbering not a sound could be heard. Why, you've never seen anything like it in your life. The crowd looked over at Mrs. Barber, set their ciders and rums down and began to clap their hands. They'd been sitting around sipping and all the time thinking the worst, and they'd hardly imagined something as simple as a horse drawn sleigh answering their prayers. The applause filled the room.

But then, leave it to Marty to throw a genuine wet dishtowel on the moment.

"Horses can pull the sled—that's for sure. The sled can ride the snow—that's for sure," Marty said.

"Marty!" Mrs. Barber said. "Don't be mealy-mouthed, and don't be beating around no bushes, lad."

"Yeah," Conway barked. "Spit it out."

"This here is dairy-farm country, Marty said. "There ain't no streetlamps in dairy farm country, and I don't care how good a team of horses is. We'd never make our way that far in the dark not knowing where the road is."

"They'll be a full moon tonight," Randy said.

"Won't be a full moon if the snow's still coming down," Marty said.

*Crack, crack, crack, crack.*

"Dale!" Mrs. Barber sparked. "You, Mayor, and Randy go pull the sleigh down like I told you. Tidy her up in the lower bay. Do it quick and hook a wagon up to our tractor. Then the three of you— you're going to string lights from the plane strip all the way over to the Gaines's place, Marty and the horses can make their way. And that'll be that!"

"No offense, Gertrude," Mike Shea said. "It may be the rum talking, dear, but that's more than a two-mile jaunt and I haven't yet seen a cord stretch that far, and I surely don't have that many lights in the store if one did."

"Dang it," the doc said.

"Oh, you'd be welcome to them if I did, but they just don't exist. Not that many," Mike Shea said.

At that, Mrs. Barber first felt she had to clear her good name.

"Mike Shea, don't you be suggesting I'm on the rum."

"Well, I wasn't…" he started.

"Firstly, good folks know I do not imbibe, and secondly and apparently, despite what the Lord gave you in height, Mike Shea, and in business know-how, excepting your gas prices are too high, the Lord missed giving you common sense."

"Well, I wasn't meaning—" Mike Shea started.

"Just in case those in this room can't remember, even though you've all been here on this farm near every year since I can remember for the harvest hayride and dance—"

"We love it," Mayor said. "The whole Crown comes."

"Well, it just so happens we have in the hayloft of the feed barn the near eighty kerosene lanterns we use to decorate the hayride and barn dance? They'll burn a half ounce per hour."

"Well, I'll be," the doc said.

"Dale," Mrs. Barber said. "After you boys get the bobsled down and rigged, go to the feed barn and pull all the lanterns down and put two ounces of kerosene in each."

"Yes, Ma."

"And take Randy and Mayor with you and go string them on fence posts from the airstrip right through the hamlet and then all down the road to the Gaines's farm."

"Should we—" Barber said.

"And light them before you hang them," Mrs. Barber said, anticipating his question. "Stay with them until you know the burn is good."

"Better hang them on fence posts all the way to Big Mike's place so Marty can drop off Don, Mary, Holbrook, and Tall Jerry there," Duba said.

"Drop Aaron by at our place," Allen said.

"Who's Aaron?" Marty asked.

"Aaron is the girl's brother. He may be flying the plane," Allen said.

"Take plenty of stick matches," Mr. Barber said. "One drive the tractor. One set in the wagon and be lighting the lanterns and handing them out to the one hanging them. It should go smooth. Make sure you stretch them out. Remember that they need to guide the horses, not light up the whole hamlet."

The room was silent again, and a sense of awe seemed to flow through the crackling of the burning fireplace. Such challenges in a difficult evening were made possible to be overcome by a mug of cider and a moment shared between friends.

*Crack, crack, crack, crack.*

"Let's get going," Mrs. Barber said. "Conway, you and your team take Dick, Duba, and Jimmy Dwyer and head up to Moore's place and get the smudge pots. Don't forget to light them. Ask him how, so you don't be setting yourselves ablaze. Dale, you and your team go get the bobsled down and all the lanterns and go hang them all. Take a roll of hay-bale string, case you need it."

"Why the string, Mom?" Barber asked.

"To tie the lantern to the post," Conway said.

"Oh," Barber said.

"Marty, you go with the doc. Harness Farmer Parker's horses and bring them over. Put them in the cow barn until we need them. They'll be warm in there. Give them some hay."

Mr. Barber interrupted with a long, warm smile and then lifted and lowered his mug of flavored cider in a toast to the love of his life.

"A toast, gentlemen!" Mr. Barber said.

Every mug in the room went up.

"To my bride," he said.

Mrs. Barber's face turned a beet red.

"Why, woman," Mr. Barber said. "You sure cut up that Tom turkey in mighty short order. My goodness, we're all proud of you."

Mrs. Barber smiled and set her ladle down.

"Whoever said a woman couldn't run the show ain't never been to a farm," she said. "Now go on, everybody, and git. Lots to do before they get here."

The room started to clear as people unfolded into groups.

"And Merry Christmas!" Mrs. Barber said.

# CHAPTER 26

## TENSIONS GROW

Passing through clouds over the heart of West Virginia, the B-25 climbed and took them to ten thousand feet.

"Looks like we'll be following the Blue Ridge Mountains awhile," Don squawked through the mic. "Then it'll be over the Pennsylvania mountains on up to Binghamton."

Aaron had both hands gripping the wheel. He was comfortable with the smoothness of the ride. He felt good with his friend Don sharing the cockpit.

"We'll be fine," Aaron said. "But the snowcaps on those mountaintops make me think there'll be some weather ahead. We can handle it."

"Reminds me of the Eighth," Don said.

"The Eighth?" Aaron asked. "You mean the Eighth Army Air Corps?"

"Some of the pilots who flew deep into Germany to drop their loads and then turn back in daylight would take the long way back. They'd chance a fly around and come back over the Alps," Don said. "Little or no flak over the Alps."

"That all must have been somethin'," Aaron said. "That surely must have been somethin'."

"You're as good as the best I've ever flown with, my friend," Don said. "You're right up there with the best."

Aaron pursed his lips and looked ahead into the horizon with a sparkle in his eyes. Then he smiled. He was ready to set the heading on zero-one-zero degree bearing north...the home stretch.

211

"Might as well keep her at ten thousand," Don said. "We'll give those mountain peaks down there plenty of room to clear under us. No telling how tall they are."

In the back of the plane Mary was trying to get Anna Kristina to rest with the racket and the bouncing of the plane.

"Ow! Anna Kristina grimaced.

"They're only bumps on clouds," Mary said.

The plane bucked twice, both times leaving them with a weightless feeling until it settled. Holbrook and Jerry bundled them both with the mattress, folding it around them. They wrapped a tarp around them, figuring the girl's combined body heat inside would keep them warm. Mary held Anna Kristina's hand and told her stories about the Pompey Hollow Book Club. She told how they saved bunnies when they were ten. She told about the bad guys they caught—the store burglars, the escaped POW guys and the pickpocket.

Anna Kristina had no idea of where they were taking her or what was in store for her, but that wasn't important to her now, it seemed.

"It hurts, Mary," Anna Kristina said.

"We'll be there soon. Then no more bumps," Mary said.

Anna Kristina knew her baby would be safe when they landed, and she was good with that. She never took her eyes off Mary's face. She listened intently to her words, almost as if Mary were her momma and telling her a bedtime story. Anna Kristina was older than Mary by two and a half years on the calendar, but she was still a child—a wonderful, eager-to-learn child. With every story she was building trust in her new friend. At one point during a pause in a story, she looked over at Mary, catching her eye.

"I 'spose this book club is...well...like a body would have to be a real somethin' to get in a club like that."

"What do you mean?" Mary asked.

"Well...I don't know. Oh, never mind. Just me bein' silly."

"Anna Kristina, are you asking me if you could join the club?"

"I didn't mean no dis—"

"Didn't anybody tell you?" Mary asked, interrupting her.

"Tell me?" Anna Kristina whispered. "Tell me what?"

"Why, young lady, Holbrook, Jerry, and me, we're the club, and we came all the way down to Little Rock just to protect you. Do you know what that means?"

"No," Anna Kristin whispered.

"Holbrook, tell Anna Kristina what that means."

"It means you're automatically in the club," Holbrook said.

Anna Kristina's eyes widened. "Is that true?"

"Absolutely!" Jerry said.

"It's official!" Mary said. "Show her, guys."

Holbrook and Jerry gave her a thumbs-up.

"Welcome to the club," Jerry said.

"You mean people like me can—"

"Why, listen to you," Mary grumbled. "Carrying on and all like you didn't know. Why yes, girl, we need people who are just like us in the club. The more the merrier and you're just like us, Anna Kristina. We could tell that right off. You're one of us!"

Anna Kristina's big, beautiful eyes glistened with tears of wonderment.

Mary looked away and puffed a curl from over her eye. She turned her head back.

"Well, are you in?" Mary asked.

"Huh?" Anna Kristina muttered.

"Are you in or not," Mary asked.

She looked Anna Kristina in the eye.

Anna Kristina smiled a yes, squeezed Mary's hand, and closed her eyes to dream. She fell asleep somewhere over the foothills of the Pennsylvania mountains.

Up in Delphi, the smudge pots had been brought down from the Moore's cider farm. They were all set in place and burning, throwing off tongues of flames lapping at the winds. The snow had stopped falling, and the glow of a full moon blanketed the valley with a silent carpet of snow. Myrtie had been alerted of the situation and was listening for the shortwave, just in case. Glowing kerosene lanterns dotted the fences all the way from the airstrip down on Oran Delphi Road up through the hamlet, over past the Gaines's place and then down to Big Mike's and Missus's Delphi Falls.

Those who weren't standing around the smudge pots, keeping warm by them, or riding with Conway while they matted down the airstrip, were either in the Barber house, sitting by the fire waiting, or up at the church, rehearsing for the services later that evening. Everyone, whether near the pasture airfield or in the Barber's, waited in the silence, listening.

They were listening for the sounds of a B-25 bomber.

Mrs. Barber held young Bobby on her lap on the rocker and began to read aloud.

*"The moon on the breast of the new-fallen snow gave a luster of midday to objects below."* Her voice was soft and as warm, just as was the wonderful tale.

That's when it came.

It first came with a rattling of tea cups and saucers on kitchen shelves. Rumbling sounds came from off in the distance at first—no one could tell from where. The sounds grew louder until the ground itself vibrated. The stately old farmhouse shivered.

The plane they all had waited for was above them, fifteen hundred feet in the air and flying directly over the Barbers' house.

*Varoom!*

It passed over with a rush of sound.

"That's them," Marty yelled. "They're coming north up from DeRuyter Lake. I thought they were supposed to be coming across Route 20, turning south on the Cherry Valley."

"They're in trouble, then," Barber said.

With that, those in the house except Bobby grabbed a coat and ran outside. Mrs. Barber scurried out behind them in her house dress and Christmas apron. They ran into the middle of Oran Delphi Road to watch for the plane, which had disappeared. A few of them were waiting to hear the crash.

No crash came.

"Dale," Mrs. Barber said. "Run inside and get my coat and some galoshes! Tell Bobby to stay put. Marty, you go get the horses and pull the sleigh rig out here."

"Shouldn't we wait here?" Marty asked.

"Wait for what?" Mrs. Barber asked. "We know they're here. They'll be landing any time now and a little girl needs help—and fast. Git!"

Marty skipped off, running to the old hay barn to pull the team of horses out. They were hitched up and waiting for him.

"Randy. You, Dale, and Mayor run down to the airstrip. Go on foot in case they need you," Mrs. Barber said. "We'll pick you up if we catch up. Go on, now."

"Are you going, too, Ma?" Barber asked.

"The girl's in girl trouble, son. She needs a woman. Go down and help them—git!"

As Marty pulled the horse team and sleigh onto Oran Delphi Road and stopped, they saw for the first time the B-25 coming back up over the center of the road at about one thousand feet.

Inside the B25, the plane was tumbling, bouncing and tipping in banks.

Tall Jerry fell to the floor and grabbed a metal frame.

"What's happening?" Anna Kristina asked, a shudder in her voice.

"Holbrook!" Mary shouted. "Grab our mattress, don't let us fall over!"

"Grab something to hang on to back there!" Don shouted.

Holbrook wrapped his arms partly around the folded mattress.

215

"We gonna to crash?" Anna Kristina cried.

Jerry crawled and reached Holbrook's hand to help stabilize the mattress.

"We're not going to crash. They're finding out where to land," Mary said.

Anna Kristina clutched Mary's hands in hers, pursed her lips in tears.

On the ground Marty and the horse team pulled onto the road.

"Look! They've circled around and coming back," Marty yelled. "That's what they've done, by golly. They were just checking out the runway."

Pointing out the cockpit window, Aaron shouted, "There she is, Don. What say we make another pass around and then land this lady?"

"Roger that, Captain," Don said. "Let 'em know the bombers are here!"

The B25 leveled out and began descending in a slow, steady dive, the burning smudge pots at the base of the landing field were in sight.

Mrs. Barber climbed into the sleigh and sat on its bench.

Marty—the best horsemen in the crown—took the reins in firm handgrips and in one motion brought the straps down on the rumps of Sarge and Sally with a gentle clap.

"Giddyap! Ktch, ktch. Let's go, you hosses!"

The horses worked up from a light stepping through the snow to a cadence with the sleigh gliding effortlessly behind them. Marty calculated by eye where the center of the road was and the fence line and followed the glow of lanterns, hurrying down toward the base of the landing strip.

Marty would shout "gee!" for the team to guide left and "haw" for the team to guide right.

FLUMP...FLUMP...FLUMP, the muffled hooves marched in the unplowed snow, their hooves packing snow each time one landed. Steam snorting from their velvet nostrils, the horses seemed to have full confidence in Marty's hand, and they welcomed the warming stretch of their legs on such a cold night.

*Varoom!*

This time the B-25 banked to the west of Oran Delphi Road to begin its approach. Aaron and Don had to get good visuals, so to circle twice for them meant they could study the best approach.

Outside on the ground, the bobsled hauling Mrs. Barber and Marty reached the base of the airstrip and turned onto the snow-covered airfield just as the B-25 roared down toward the field, passing about twenty feet above the smudge pots.

Inside the plane Aaron shouted back, "Hang on back there, it's going to be a bumpy landing!"

As the plane cleared the burning pots to touch down, Marty slapped the reins.

"Haw! Haw! Haw! Giddyap now, Hosses!"

Sarge and Sally broke into a gallop and the sleigh swerved right, sliding around on the packed snow and it speeded up to reach the moving plane, which touched down, engines whining, and rolled to a bumpy stop.

Inside, Don was making suggestions.

"Aaron, we might shut her down to save fuel. She still has to make it back to Binghamton to fuel up."

"Roger that," Aaron said.

Don looked out the cockpit window and saw the Minneapolis Moline tractor and the plow at the edge of the field.

"Looks like that tractor over there has all we'll need to turn this lady around when the time comes for takeoff," Don said.

With that, they went through the shutdown sequence, switching off switches and checking gauges. Aaron unstrapped his harness, turned in his seat and stepped into the back cargo area first. Don following behind him.

"How you making it back here?" Aaron asked with a smile. "Everybody doin' okay?"

"That landing was so cool!" Jerry said.

"Well, we're here!" Mary said. "We're finally here! Yay!"

She handed Anna Kristina tissues to wipe her tears.

"We're safe, Anna," Mary said.

Jerry helped Holbrook unwrap the girls from the tarp and the mattress. Don stepped into the rear compartment.

"Stand back and stay clear," Don said.

He pulled the lever that lowered the bomb-bay doors, which constituted much of the floor of the plane. Aaron knelt and, leaning on his side, stuck his head down and out. He watched Marty pull the team of horses and the bobsled up just outside the reach of the starboard wing.

Since he'd been based in Detroit during the war, Aaron was no stranger to snowstorms. He gathered the chocks and dropped them through the opening. He was certain the plane wouldn't roll on the snowy hayfield, but procedure was procedure.

"Holbrook, Tall Jerry," he said. "Drop the tarps down. Let's get a team to help cover the engines. Tie them on with a good seal. We don't need moisture in the engines or on the sparks."

He lowered the ladder.

"Miss Mary, will you help Anna Kristina down? I think your chariot awaits," Aaron said.

Mary and Anna Kristina made their way down the ladder.

"Are you all right, Anna?" Mary asked at the bottom of the ladder.

"I'm okay," Anna Kristina said.

They walked over to the sleigh.

"Hello, honey," Mrs. Barber said. "Climb in with me, where it's warm."

"Are you Aunt Lucy?" Anna Kristina asked.

"No, honey, I'm Mrs. Barber. Aunt Lucy is at church. It'll be Christmas tomorrow, ya know, dear."

"I know," Anna Kristina said as she stepped over the side rail of the bobsled and sat next to Mrs. Barber.

"Santa already give'd me a present," Anna Kristina said.

Mrs. Barber saw the whole day and that evening as a blessing from the Lord—almost as a miracle for this child. She looked at the girl's personal "Santa" moment through her own eyes, just as if the safe airplane landing alone was a gift from Santa.

"Oh, I just know he did," Mrs. Barber said as she wrapped a blanket around the girl and pulled her close. "I just know Santa did that, honey."

Mary sat in front. She turned around so that she could face them.

Anna Kristina looked over at Mary and whispered, "He did."

Mary smiled.

Inside the airplane, after all the tarps had been dropped to the ground, Aaron looked about for last-minute details.

"Holbrook and Tall Jerry," Aaron said. "You climb down first."

The two climbed out, purposely taking their time stepping down the rungs of the ladder, taking in the sights and inhaling the smells of this once-in-a-lifetime memory.

"You next, Don," Aaron said.

Don saluted Aaron.

"After you, Captain!" Don said.

Aaron looked up and smiled. He nodded his head as though to thank Don for the respect, returned the salute, and stepped down the ladder. With that, Don cranked up the bomb-bay doors. He then let himself down the boarding passage and closed that once he was out.

Don looked about.

"Folks? Everyone?"

"Listen up," Duba shouted.

"Thanks for all your help," Don said. "The strip was perfect. I'd like you to meet Aaron here—US Army Air Force, our pilot-captain tonight. And over there is his sister, Anna Kristina."

Dick, Duba, Conway, and Dwyer were hovering around the B-25, staring up at it and soaking it in like they were in a dream.

Aaron started to ask for help with the chocks and tarps. Dick saw him and anticipated his thought.

"You guys go on," Dick said. "We'll take care of the plane."

"But, it's important that—" Aaron started.

"You go on, now," Conway said. "We'll cover the engines and chock her."

"You might snuff the smudge pots out, so they don't draw too much attention," Don said.

"We plan to," Duba said. "We're going to load them up after we finish with the plane and take them back to Moore's, where they belong, tonight. We have the lids to snuff them out with."

Don and Aaron stepped through the snow and climbed onto the sleigh. They sat behind Mrs. Barber and Anna Kristina. Holbrook and Tall Jerry sat backward behind them with their legs stuck up over the back of the sled. Randy, Mayor, and Barber stayed at the smudge pots to help.

"Let's get this little lady home by a warm fire where she belongs," Mrs. Barber said.

Marty raised the straps and lowered them firmly onto the rumps of the horses.

"Giddyap!" he snapped. "Let's go, you hosses."

The sleigh lurched forward.

"Gee!" Marty said. "Gee!"

The horses bore left, pulling the sled in a large circle around the B-25 with riders looking up at it—the bulging engines, the cockpit, and the stout wings. It was a sight the Delphi hamlet would never forget. The plane was a reminder of a war they had lived through, but the young had only heard on the radio or seen on the Saturday morning picture-show newsreels.

Wasn't long before Marty was shouting back, "Hang on!"

The sleigh made it over the side-road gulley with a jump up onto Oran Delphi Road, and headed toward the hamlet. Marty could see the kerosene lanterns on the fence posts up ahead at the edge of the hamlet, helping to guide him. The "*flump, flump, flump*" of hooves marched on in the unplowed snow.

Marty cocked his head around. "Don, I thought the plan was that you were going to fly in over Cherry Valley, coming in on Route 20 from Lafayette and turn in from the north. What happened to that?"

"Fog," Aaron said. "That whole hilltop was covered in fog. We couldn't get a good visual."

"We couldn't see where Route 11 and Route 20 come together," Don said. "Like the man said, thick fog."

"What'd you wind up doing?" Marty asked.

"I knew Cazenovia Lake," Don said. "And I knew the DeRuyter Lake. We decided to take her up to five thousand feet, where we could see better and look around. Once we found DeRuyter Lake, I had Aaron follow Oran Delphi north all the way up. Tall Jerry told me the Barber's place was the first farm on the right outside the hamlet, so once we got a visual on those big barns, everything made sense."

"We saw the fire barrels and were sure we found it," Aaron said. "What a welcome sight they were. The rest was easy, after a couple of flyovers."

Sitting backwards, Mary, Holbrook, and Jerry looked at the scene they were leaving behind. The smudge pots were still blazing, burning lifetime memories into their night. Mary leaned forward and held Anna Kristina's right hand. Anna Kristina shivered in the cold as she held Mrs. Barber's left hand. She watched the barns and homes they passed by as the sleigh entered the hamlet, her trip nearly over.

## CHAPTER 27

## CHRISTMAS IS HERE,
## NEW FRIENDS ARE NEAR

The moon framed the hamlet with a hallowed glow from a carpet of snow blanketing the roads, yards, and rooftops. There were reading lamps behind draped windows and colorful lights strung on porches as the horse-drawn sleigh glided past neighbors, one by one. There were lighted candles on windowsills and holly wreaths on front doors. Five snowmen on that many yards stood watch for happy childhood memories and photo album snapshots they would one day become. The north star seemed to rest just above the church steeple as if it was the star the wise men followed the night Jesus was born. The tree decorated in front of the church, bright with cheery Christmas lights, survived the storm. Every window of the church was aglow with a warm, golden-yellow light. They sledded on past it all.

As the sleigh glided by the church, Marty turned around.

"Here?" Marty asked.

Mrs. Barber looked at the church.

"Let's g'wan and take her home to the Gaines's place first," Mrs. Barber said. "No sense stopping and risking getting caught in another snowstorm."

"Ktch, ktch," Marty sounded. He slapped the reins gently down on the rumps of Sarge and Sally.

They were turning onto Delphi Falls Road to head down to the Gaines's farm, when Anna Kristina shouted, "Oh no!"

"What is it dear?" Mrs. Barber asked.

"I don't know."

"Nothing to be afraid of, honey. We just turned a corner, is all. We're here with you."

"Are you okay?" Mary asked.

Mrs. Barber opened the front of the blanket that was folded around Anna Kristina. She unbuttoned her coat to find a note safety-pinned to her sweater. She opened and read it.

"Honey, your water broke early this morning."

"What's happening?" Anna Kristina asked in a voice that matched fear in her eyes. She flinched over again.

"They just start, honey?"

"On the airplane."

"I just thought she was afraid of the bumps," Mary said.

"Marty!" Mrs. Barber snapped.

"Yo!" Marty shouted.

"Back up, son. Back us up, quick. You've got to get us over to the church as fast as you can."

"Whoa!" Marty barked.

The team of horses stopped instantly, scuffing hoofs of snow, exhaling steam from their nostrils.

"Back!" Marty shouted. "Back! Back! Back!"

Once again in the middle of Oran Delphi Road, Marty barked new orders.

"Haw, team, haw. Giddyap!"

Sarge and Sally lurched to a near gallop, guiding the sled back through the hamlet. In front of the church, Marty pulled hard on the reins.

"Whoa!"

Don and Aaron jumped from the back of the sleigh. They each put an arm around Anna Kristina's back and clasping their hands together, they lifted and cradled her. They carried her past the tall Christmas tree in front, twinkling through snow-covered lights and colorful Christmas balls and up the steps of the historic church. Holbrook pulled the door.

Mrs. Barber got from the sleigh to the church and stepped in quickly. She called for calm, with folks inside wondering what the commotion was. She shouted her announcement for help from the full choir, who had an otherwise fairly empty church because of the weather.

"We're having a baby!" Mrs. Barber shouted.

In 1953 a farm woman wouldn't need to hear another word or an ounce of direction following that declaration. Having babies was as natural to them as was dying on the farm.

"Keep singing, ladies," Judy Clancy offered. "A baby is born tonight. Sing!"

"Hallelujah!" the choir cried out in unison.

The Davenport girl sat at the piano and led the choir into a litany of Christmas songs. Mrs. Barber signaled for Jackie and Alda to come meet Anna Kristina. As they approached, they both looked down and smiled at their new friend.

"Can we get Anna Kristina a cushion to lie on, Mrs. Barber?" Alda asked.

"That's a nice thought, dear," Mrs. Barber said. "Boys, help the girls get two of the church-bench cushions over here and let's get them under this pretty girl."

They comforted Anna Kristina, Alda and Jackie each holding her hands. Mary and Aunt Lucy nudged over.

"Anna Kristina," Mary said. "This is Aunt Lucy."

"Merry Christmas, pretty girl," Aunt Lucy said.

Anna Kristina looked up and smiled, trying to take it all in. Then she looked into young Alda's eyes. She looked at Jackie. She looked back at Aunt Lucy's smile.

She groaned again, holding her tummy.

Aaron leaned over and set a pillowcase with her belongings next to her for comfort.

In the background the choir sang *Silent Night*.

Anna Kristina looked up into Mary's eyes. She reached out for her hand.

"Where am I?" she whispered.

"You're almost home," Mary said.

"Am I going to die?"

"Oh no, dear," Aunt Lucy said. "You're going to live. That baby inside you is going to live."

"Why, child, you have blessed our Christmas just by being here with us tonight," Mrs. Barber said.

"You are home, little sister, and you are free," Aaron said.

Anna Kristina lifted her hand over to her pillowcase. She rummaged inside and felt around under the cotton cloth.

"I already seen Santa," she said.

"You have?" Jackie asked.

"He had a white beard."

"Did you see him in a store window?" Mary asked.

"No," Anna Kristina said. "He was the man what drive'd me to the hospital, but we didn't get there. Honest."

Don smiled at Tall Jerry.

Anna Kristina pulled two packages from her pillow sack. She looked at Jerry, made certain he was Tall Jerry and handed him a package.

"This is for you," she said. "That man said he was Saint Nicholas. That's what Santa's real name is, he told me."

"Hemingway," Jerry whispered to himself.

Anna Kristina cramped up with a whimpered moan. The ladies asked the men to step away as they went about their business. The breathing and moaning sounded painful, but it was necessary. Just as the choir was rejoicing behind the organ's rumbling crescendo celebrating the birth of Jesus, the new baby spat out a cry, letting the world know that he was there, and he was cold. Mrs. Barber handed him to Aunt Lucy, who swaddled the infant and laid him softly on Anna Kristina's breast.

"What'cha going to name such a beautiful little baby boy?" Aunt Lucy asked.

"Such a handsome baby," Mrs. Barber said.

"He got a name yet, Anna Kristina?" Mary asked.

"Nicholas," Anna Kristina whispered as she lifted the baby to her face. She kissed him ever so gently.

"Hello my Nicholas," she whispered.

*A white Christmas in the Crown.*

# EPILOGUE

Merry Christmas!

Tall Jerry's gift from the Saint Nicholas who drove Anna Kristina to the Arkansas diner in Carlisle was a copy of the book *The Old Man and the Sea*, by Ernest Hemingway himself. He had autographed it and written in it, *"To my friend Tall Jerry. Signed, 'Papa' (Manolin Santiago)."*

Don saw the autograph and smiled. He knew then who the mystery man at the Capital Hotel was.

Like ole Charlie here, Don is gone now, but he was proud of the Thanksgiving and Christmas he spent with Tall Jerry. He would say to Jerry, "It's almost as if your guardian angel orchestrated that whole thing."

Ernest Hemingway's gift to Anna Kristina was a copy of the same book. He autographed hers, too.

*"It's good to have an end to a journey, but it is the journey that matters in the end, young lady. Signed, Your friends, St. Nicholas and Ernest Hemingway."*

Anna Kristina and her son, Nicholas, finished school as members of the Gaines family. They both went to college and became teachers, as did Alda and Jackie. Each are a happy part of the Gaines family to this day.

Ernest Hemingway flew to Africa for a wild game hunt. In the course of a year he was injured in two airplane crashes. Eight years later he got the cancer, like ole Charlie here. Mr. Hemingway is with God now.

This story is a Delphi Falls gift to you. Ole Charlie here hopes it makes a difference in your life. I hope it helps set an example and you make a difference in other people's lives.

It's not too late to start. Merry Christmas.

*A world citizen, Hemingway fought for equality*

*Jackie and Alda's grade in the Crown*

## MESSAGE FROM THE AUTHOR

It's up to us. Try to remember my favorite passage…

("We spent hundreds of years setting bad examples, teaching grade school children wrong by those examples," Big Mike said.

"Had we spent the years since the Civil War teaching grade school children what's right would have been our saying we're sorry," Mike Shea said.

"How would that do it?" the doc asked.

"The kids in the 1860s would have integrated on their own steam." Big Mike said.

"This sort of thing can only be taught," Mike Shea said.)

…it begins on the very first day of school.  It has to be taught. You have to insist that your schools teach it beginning on day one.

JMA